CW01501993

The two vehicles slowly nosed their way up the wadi. In the lead was a modified Land Rover, followed at a distance by a rather large truck of unknown origin. Receding into the distance behind them was Mount Hor. To the east could be seen glimpses of a bleak wilderness, and to the west stretched the Gulf of Suez.

Seven travel-stained tourists wearily took in the view, as their vehicle slowly approached the next campsite. Although they were all hardened travelers, today's rougher ride had unexpectedly tired them. They were in need of a rest and, what was more important, an opportunity to stretch their legs. However, in their minds they were as anxious as ever to explore the next archaeological site on the schedule, which had been prepared for them as part of the "In the Footsteps of Moses" tour.

The vehicles drew up to a few sparse palm trees that hinted of a nearby water supply and parked on a clearly marked flat area. The director of the tour was first to leap out of the Land Rover. He turned and gave his now familiar call, "OK, everybody out!" As the weary seven emerged onto the sand, he continued, "We are camping here tonight. Everyone pick up your fresh water supply from the support wagon while the crew sets up your tents."

The tourists stretched themselves, and as they slowly made their way to the supply wagon, two of them broke away from the group to relieve themselves behind a palm tree. As the tourists sipped carefully from their precious water supply, they observed the crew frantically setting up camp in its usual rectangular shape, with sleeping quarters on one side and the "office" and crew's quarters on the opposite side.

A fire was lit and prepared dishes were placed on a cooking frame. Very soon the dishes were simmering over the flames. The pre-dinner drink was given out to the seven now reclining on camp chairs. All was becoming calm and more civilized. In a relatively short time, they were able to help themselves to the hot dishes and delights of a buffet meal, which had become for them the highlight of the day. As they relaxed, the seven became a lot more sociable toward each other and the director.

After the meal, the road-weary men had time to tidy their things, wash, and freshen up; then they gathered in the director's office. The office was comprised of a simple awning with a central makeshift table. The director was still in a rather sharp mood. Perhaps he, too, was tired. "Continuing on their journey," he paused to ensure that his guests were paying attention, "following their escape from Egypt, the Hebrews under their leader, Moses, reached the area we now occupy." He pointed to a map on the table and continued, "As we saw yesterday, Aaron died on top of Mount Horeb. At this point in their epic journey, the Hebrews became angry with Moses, God, and with their whole situation. They were tired of the manna

NEHUSHTAN

NEHUSHTAN

WILLIAM WORLEY

ANOMALOS PUBLISHING HOUSE

CRANE

Anomalos Publishing House, Crane 65633
© 2008 by William Worley
All rights reserved. Published 2008
Printed in the United States of America
08   1
ISBN-10: 098150910X (paper)

EAN-13: 9780981509105 (paper)

Cover illustration and design by Steve Warner

A CIP catalog record for this book is available from the Library of
Congress.

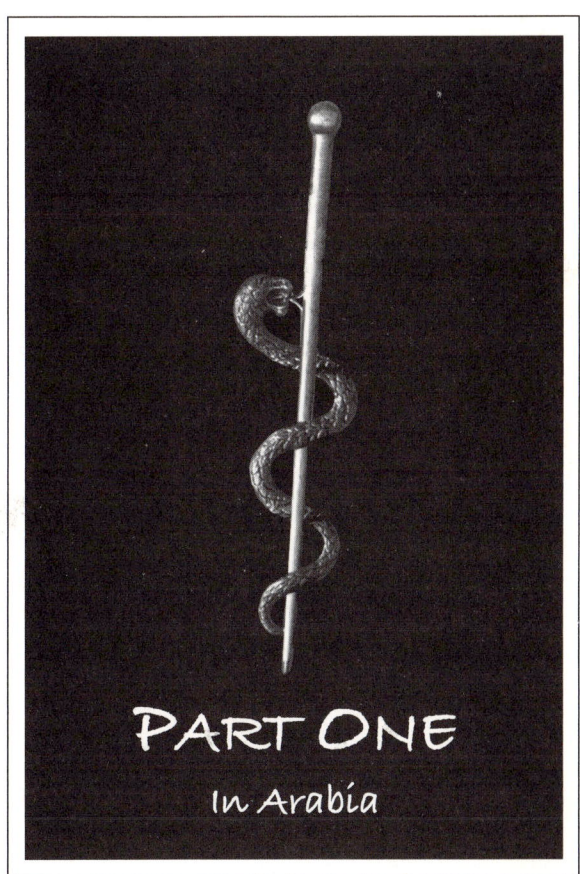

PART ONE

In Arabia

and were becoming anxious about their water supply. They felt that they had relied too heavily on Moses to meet their need for water. They complained so much that they were punished by the Lord, the God of Israel, who sent fiery serpents in amongst them."

"What fiery serpents would they have been?" interrupted Fred Wiseman, an American scholar of very high reputation and obvious Jewish descent. "There have never been any animals that breathed fire. That is just a fable. Snakes I can live with, but fire-breathing serpents I don't go along with." There was a murmur of approval from the company.

"Listen," said the director in an even tone, "I have led this tour for many years. I tell all the tourists what I am telling you now. I talk about what your Bible says, and sometimes I can show you a few extra things that the Bible doesn't mention. Fiery serpents were recorded, and so fiery serpents are what you get. Proving their existence is not my business. OK?"

A dumb silence followed. This particular band of tourists was proving to be a bit of a handful for the director, especially since they appeared to be more informed than the usual groups. A few, like Wiseman, were set on making life difficult. The director's abrasive attitude was not helping the harmony of the group.

"Continuing then?" He paused for assurance and support from the seven tourists. "The Hebrew people became plagued by these fiery serpents, so within a few days, many people died. Then, as the Hebrews began to realize the error of their ways, Moses was instructed by the Lord to make an image of a fiery serpent out of brass. He then affixed it to the top of a pole, so that whenever a person who had been bitten by these serpents looked upon the brass serpent, they would be healed."

"A great story, I am sure," said Ike Moor, "but what happened to the brass serpent then?"

Responding to renewed interest in the topic, the director effused enthusiasm. "There is another reference to the brass serpent somewhere in the Old Testament and also a passing reference to it in the New Testament. It's a bit like the search for the Ark of the Covenant. No one really knows where that Ark is now, do they? However, there is amongst the local inhabitants hereabouts a tradition, or maybe is it just a continued rumor, that the brass serpent was made to meet a specific danger—a danger not evident anywhere else on Earth. Some say that the brass serpent is still here, held in this area for some future outbreak, which many feel will occur." There was an uneasy shuffling amongst the seven.

"And some say that's a load of hogwash," interrupted Fred. "Look, I need to do some urgent work on my research into the flora and fauna of this region, so how long are we here?"

"Yes, this is a good area for general investigation," said the director, "so we can afford two nights here, if it meets with your approval." The company nodded their approval in a more friendly fashion. "One final word then," said the director. "This area is not exactly safe. There are people out there who are more dangerous than any fiery serpents, so no going out alone. We do have the latrine positioned beside the shower area. Please use it," he said, glancing across at those who had relieved themselves elsewhere. "And of course, breakfast as usual at sunup. Have a good rest."

The group dispersed slowly to their assigned tents. Some paired off to moan and complain further about the director and his rough presentation of the tour.

2

Major William Jones, RAMC, sat quietly on his camp
bed. He completed his daily journal as quickly as
possible and then turned to his small, black Bible. He read a
passage briefly and then placed it back amongst his few belongings. He found his wallet, opened it, and gazed at the picture of
his wife and two children framed on one side. Then he glanced
across to the other side of his wallet, where his old military
insignia of a brass serpent coiled around a pole was kept. He
stared at the object for quite a while, recalling many memories.
Several moments later, he put the items away, slowly removed
his boots, and spread his long, lean body out on the bed frame.
Immediately he dropped off to sleep.

Jones fell into a deep sleep, his body needing the rest.
As the events of the day played upon his memory, he began
to dream. A white knight in shining armor carrying a white
shield with a red cross upon it was mounted on a huge horse.
Together horse and rider were going forth looking for worthy
challengers. Suddenly, the challenger was there confronting
them. It was a black knight, "Bible black" from head to toe,

mounted on a black horse and carrying a dark shield on which was painted a bronze snake.

The opponents raised their lances in acknowledgement of each other and then plunged furiously forward. They clashed together, and their momentum threw them apart again. They whirled around to see what damage they had done to each other. Nothing? Again they hurled themselves towards each other, lances shattering on shields. No damage was evident. The two knights drew their huge swords, and with these weapons they renewed their combat. They cut and thrust at each other from their mounted positions, the horses wheeling and turning at their masters' wills.

The black knight's horse turned more slowly than that of the white knight. After a few passes, the white knight abruptly turned his horse and came up behind the black knight before he could complete his turn. The white knight's great sword swung over the top of the shield of the black knight, cutting into the joint of helmet and armor.

The black knight fell from his horse, and as he fell, his foot remained caught in the horse's stirrup. His horse floundered on, towing the black knight's body behind it. The battle was over.

Hardly had the white knight gained his victory when human faces confronted him. A multitude of voices cried out to him, "Help us! Please, help us! We need a champion to fight against the evil one." The white knight was waved onward toward a distant foe. All of a sudden he was confronted by a large, fiery dragon—a real dragon with nasty claws and scales. What was worse, there was fire emanating from its mouth. The knight took in the view with just one glance, and he knew within himself that he could not overcome such a huge monster. He turned away, looking for a means of escape from the situation he faced. As he turned, he was again confronted by the people. They cried out in desperation, "Help us! Help us!"

Once again the white knight turned to face his foe. Strangely, the dragon appeared a little smaller, perhaps only two meters high and five meters long. A fresh lance appeared in the white knight's hand. He urged his horse toward the dragon but kept well away from its fiery mouth as he rode past. He tried another quick pass as the dragon slowly turned towards him, keeping well clear of the flames emanating from its mouth. His horse appeared fearless, but he himself could see the danger in closing in on this beast.

Once again he thrust his horse toward the dragon, but making a much closer pass this time. They came so close that he felt the heat of the flames emerging from the dragon's mouth. His mind raced through his various battles of the past. Which tactic, which method would work against this awesome beast?

He made another rapid pass near the dragon. Was the creature slowing down with each turn that it had to make? Yes! The creature was slower on its left side that its right side. Here was the opportunity. After a few more trial runs, he knew what he must do.

Lowering his lance, he charged forward, focusing on the rear left limb of the dragon. Sweeping through the flames, he slammed the lance into the flesh of that limb. He whirled the horse around to the right side of the creature as it tried to follow him around to the left. Its head swung the other way, and the flames nearly caught him as he passed.

Another lance appeared in the white knight's hand. Again he surged forward to attack the left side of the dragon. His aim was better this time, and he savagely thrust the lance into the wounded limb, pinning it to the ground. The creature roared in pain. Flames of anger belched from its mouth.

Drawing his huge sword, the white knight went in for the kill. He made a pass along the weakened left side then whirled around to the right side and slashed at the creature's underbelly with his sword. The dragon twisted in mortal pain. The white knight again wheeled his horse around to the rear of the dragon and, coming upon its neck on the left side, thrust his sword fully into it. The sword buried itself up to the hilt and stayed there. The dragon choked and roared.

The white knight swung his horse away to survey the scene; he saw that the dragon was beaten. Unable to turn or breathe, it slowly fell to the ground, where it continued to emit small puffs of smoke as its life ebbed slowly away.

When he was sure that the dragon could do no further harm, the white knight moved forward to finish it off. A new sword appeared in his hand. He approached the still feebly puffing monster and aimed a blow at the point just above the place where the first sword was embedded. This blade was extremely sharp, for with one cut the dragon's head fell from its shoulders.

All at once the same faces were pressing in on him. The people were congratulating him and clapping him on the shoulder saying, "Well done! Well done!"

"Wake up! Wake up! Major Jones!" Jones woke with a start. "Sun up! Time for breakfast, Major Jones," said the director.

Jones, now wide awake, did not rise immediately, but reached into his satchel of personal possessions. Withdrawing his wallet, he slowly opened it and gazed once more at the picture of his slim wife and their portly children. Then, his focus traveled across to the coiled serpent of the military insignia. His recent dream made no connection with what he beheld there. After a short interval, he returned the wallet to its place. Refreshed, he stooped to pull on his boots in preparation for the walk to the latrine.

There was insufficient water for a proper early morning shower at the site, so Jones returned to finish his preparations at the washbasin, which was placed conveniently just outside his tent. When all was completed, he tidied up his possessions in the tent and placed essential items for the day beside his satchel. He went outside and found that he was indeed last—last up and last in line for breakfast. The selection of leftovers from the main breakfast was limited. "Still," he thought, "a strong cup of coffee will soon sharpen my senses."

As Jones sat down to consume his breakfast, the director was already beginning his morning monologue. "Here are your maps for today. Let me repeat, I do not want you going off alone. Before you leave, please show me exactly what region you will be operating in. Today you will carry firearms, even though our tour has never experienced any trouble. In these unsettled times, it costs nothing to be more careful. Carry with you the supplies that the crew laid out for today. Although this is not the hottest time of the year, you will do well to conserve water and stay out of direct sunlight as much as possible."

He paused and then dropped his voice and asked, "Any questions? No? Then dinner is at sunset. Don't forget, please check with me before you leave the campsite." Some of the group got up immediately. Others, like Jones, were in no particular hurry.

"Major Jones!" called the director. "I have a surprise for you." As the director approached, he was closely followed by a slightly built Arab, who was dressed in flowing robes. "Major Jones, meet Nasir." Jones and Nasir acknowledged each other. "Nasir has particular knowledge of this area," continued the director, "and he is familiar with your research requirements. I thoroughly recommend him as being most loyal to me and to the In the Footsteps of Moses tour. He is always available to our tourists whenever we come into this area."

"That is most thoughtful of you, director," Jones responded.

"He has many relatives in this area, so through his contacts he can help you with your research," continued the director.

"We need to be making tracks," added Nasir in clear English.

"How are you with camels?" asked the director.

"Fine," responded Jones.

"Good," said the director. "Your camel is over there."

Nasir indicated two camels quietly squatting beside the crew's quarters. "Could you bring your equipment over to the camels, Major Jones, as soon as you are ready to go?"

"Won't take a moment," replied Jones.

He crossed the site to his tent, placed the director's revolver, food supplies, a water bottle, and a few other items into his satchel, slung it over his shoulder, and then walked toward their transportation. The two men mounted camels and moved slowly away from the campsite in an easterly direction. As they settled to the pace of travel, Nasir spoke.

"I have one or two things to show you sir—some items that may well please you. We Arabs have many traditions associated with the Hebrew people who passed through this region centuries ago."

"If you can show me something associated with the serpents of this area, I will be most interested," said Jones.

They rode in silence up a wadi and then out onto a long ridge. After awhile they came upon a pile of stones. Dismounting, Nasir showed Jones a large engraved rock, positioned at the base of the pile. "I have been told that this writing has some importance. Others have said that it is in Hebrew."

Jones peered closely at the writing, which was thickly covered with sand. Reaching into his satchel, he brought out a small brush which he gently applied to the inscription. The sand was carefully removed, revealing a Hebrew inscription.

"Death by fiery serpent," he read aloud for Nasir's benefit. "What's this?" Under the writing he could make out a picture. Jones applied his brush more vigorously to the caked sand.

"It's a snake," commented Nasir.

"Funny kind of snake," said Jones. "What's this fuzzy area under its throat? Can't really make out what it is."

He again reached for his satchel and drew out a piece of paper. He proceeded to copy exactly what was on the stone. When he was finished, Jones carefully inserted the paper into its folder. Taking the brush, he dusted around the perimeter of the inscription, looking for any other writing along the edge, but nothing was revealed. "Most interesting, Nasir," he said. "Have you anything else on this…er…same theme?"

"There is another site quite far from here that I would like to show you," said Nasir as they made their way to the camels. "I have made preparations for your visit, but I do need to warn you that we have visitors to this area who are not well disposed to foreigners. We will have to tread warily."

"I'm in your hands," said Jones.

They moved off in a more southerly direction, heading down from the ridge. After an hour's ride, as the sun become increasingly uncomfortable, their course turned due south and then changed to the west as they found a well-used track which lead eventually into a small village. Nasir was leading the way and skirted to the south of the village. They approached a sturdily built homestead, which appeared to have no surrounding fence or boundaries, but it did have commanding views of the countryside. As they neared the homestead, Nasir was spotted by a handful of children, who called out greetings as they ran forward. The noise brought adults from inside the building, and the children drew back as one distinguished man strode out purposefully to meet them.

"Greetings my son," he spoke in Arabic. "Have you brought us another foreigner to covet our possessions?"

"Not a foreigner, but a friend who comes in peace," responded Jones in Arabic.

Taken aback, Nasir responded in Arabic, "Can my father hold back his hospitality from a man who speaks our language so well?"

"The father of Nasir bids welcome to our guest. Shalom!" Nasir's father waved the children forward, who mobbed the visitors. The company, now officially welcomed, moved into the house, leaving the children outside.

Once seated and supplied with coffee, the conversation focused on the reason for Jones's visit. "Your interest in serpents is not unknown in these parts. We have had more inquiries than you would imagine," said Nasir's father. "We have a village emblem that is worthy of your attention. My son will take you to see it presently. I need to warn you, Major Jones, we have visitors to this area who are not at all friendly toward foreigners."

"Yes, so I have heard," responded Jones.

"We will try to avoid any conflict, my father," said Nasir. At this, Nasir arose abruptly from his couch, and Jones followed suit. Together they walked out of the homestead and down a rough track which opened into a dilapidated village square. The only item of any interest was a pole standing at the northern corner. As they moved toward it, Jones observed some rags hanging rather limply from the top of the pole. They drew near the pole, and a slight breeze caused the rags to flutter a little. Jones gasped as a stronger gust revealed what was under the covering. There he saw a metallic snake wrapped around the pole's short crosspiece.

"We keep it covered," said Nasir. "We don't want to arouse too much outside interest."

"What is it doing in such a public place?" asked Jones.

"You can see that it is not the original brass serpent," continued Nasir, "but it was erected as a memorial to that great event of the past. Our local chief knows a great deal about its history, so come this way, and you can meet him." Nasir led the way across to the west of the village, followed by a startled Jones, who really could not comprehend what he had just seen.

Jones thought to himself, "What is this great historical emblem doing in the middle of a rundown village?"

Nasir ushered Jones into a small dwelling occupied by a lone figure. "Greetings to you El Zohar," proclaimed Nasir loudly in Arabic. "I have brought Major Jones to visit you. He has come over many seas to meet you face to face. He is not like the other foreigners who come to spy upon our people, for he speaks our language."

"Then he is doubly welcome," responded El Zohar.

"Welcome, Major Jones. Welcome, Nasir. Welcome to my humble dwelling." El Zohar indicated that they should seat themselves upon cushions, which appeared to have been randomly scattered across the room. A rather small servant brought in the customary coffee.

Jones began the conversation cautiously. "I have a passing interest in the biblical brass serpent," he said in an interested but cautious tone to avoid displaying too much excitement over the topic. "Nasir has shown me the serpent which you have as your village emblem. Why is it that you have such a thing?"

"I will tell you all that I know about this subject," said El Zohar, "as soon as you tell me exactly why you carry a similar image in your personal belongings."

Jones gasped in amazement, "How did you know of my army insignia?"

"We Arabs know much more than you think," responded El Zohar. "Why is it that you carry such a thing with you?"

"My family has been interested in the brass serpent for many years," Jones said, feeling rather reluctant to open up to El Zohar. "We have connections with a group of historians who follow up on information on biblical artifacts. We, as a family, have in our personal research kept up to scratch with our Arabic and Hebrew languages. There are also medical reasons why our family has become particularly interested in the brass serpent." Jones reached into his satchel and brought out his wallet which he opened to reveal his RAMC military insignia. "This is a badge from my military uniform. The serpent is a symbol of healing, a symbol not unlike what our holy book says Moses erected in this very area."

"All very interesting," said El Zohar, "but come now, Major Jones. Tell me the truth, what is your real interest in all of this? What is it that you seek? What is it that you still hide from me?"

Jones hesitated for a moment, and then he committed himself to be frank with the Arab chieftain. "As I said, my family has always had an interest in the brass serpent, for it offers a means of healing for the poor unfortunates who suffer from snakebite. My problem is that my family has suffered grievously over many years from snakebites. For instance, my grandfather, Alexander William Jones, died of snakebite in the Sudan. My uncle, William Smythe Jones, died of snakebite in Cairo. Cousin James Colman, you may have heard of his research into the tombs of the Pharaohs near Cairo. He died when he, too, was bitten by something in the night. We suppose it was a snake. Then, there is my wife, Helen. She nearly died of snakebite in Beersheba. It was a miracle that she was saved."

"Now you are speaking the truth," said El Zohar.

"I carry my military insignia," continued Jones, "as a permanent reminder of man's need for healing. I served for many years in the Royal Army Medical Corps, and so my focus, my interest and that of my family has always been in healing—healing from snakebite."

"How frank you have been," said El Zohar, "and now, for my part, I will share with you what I have observed about this brass serpent of yours. You are not the first to come here looking for the healing power of the brass serpent. However, we have nothing to hide. The ancient people followed Moses through our region. Our own history tells of a serpent on a pole. Some say that after passing through here, the serpent on a pole was no longer needed by the Hebrews, and so it was left behind. It may have been left behind as both a warning to our people and as a means of healing should the scourge of snakes ever return. Our village emblem is a poor copy of what the original may have looked like. Other villages around here have the same emblem. Where the original is located, no one really knows. Moses may have taken it with him. But if he did, why would we keep the emblem?"

"I see," responded Jones. "Why then do you still display the emblem?"

"To confuse the enemy, my friend," interjected Nasir.

"One thing I can tell you," continued El Zohar, "is that there are still many types of venomous snakes in the area. Would you like to see one?"

"Yes, that would be most interesting," Jones forced himself to say. Inwardly he recoiled at the thought of being anywhere near a snake. He was shown into a small, adjacent room that possessed little furniture other than a glass case situated in one corner. Not approaching too closely, Jones observed a sizeable, chubby snake moving slowly back and forth within the case.

"It must be feeding time," said El Zohar. "Our friend is restless. Come! Take a closer look at our household pet." Jones cautiously eased himself nearer. There appeared to be a slight glow around the head of the snake. "I see that you notice the brightness around the serpent's head. We feel that this serpent is not fully grown, so how it will appear as an adult we can only guess," said El Zohar. "Would you like to see it being fed?"

Not waiting for a response, El Zohar clapped his hands,

and his servant scurried into the room carrying a medium-sized box. It was pressed against a small shutter in the glass cage. The shutter was carefully raised, and a large rat leapt into the case, hoping to find freedom. With a movement as quick as lightning, the snake struck the rat and engulfed it in one snap of its jaws.

El Zohar resumed nonchalantly, "There are other more deadly serpents in this region for us to be concerned about." Taking the tone of these words as a prompting, Jones and Nasir stood and bade farewell to the chieftain.

Nasir ushered Jones out of the house and led the way back to his own family home. "We need to be heading back now," warned Nasir after they had refreshed themselves. Jones said goodbye to the family, especially Nasir's father, thanking him for his hospitality. They remounted their camels and set off for the camp.

4

Their route was more direct this time, and after an hour and a half they neared the camp. Nasir halted abruptly, "Something is not right at the camp." He brought up a pair of binoculars to view the campsite. "No one is moving about. The crew should be well into setting up dinner by now. It's a special meal tonight with a local flavor. But there is no activity. None at all. None!"

"That is strange!" said Jones. "Stay hidden from view, and I will scout around the camp to see what I can find. Wait here until I return."

Jones slid from his camel and moved toward the west side of the camp. Nasir tethered the camels and prepared for action. After a quarter of an hour, Jones returned.

"Yes, it is ominously quiet at the camp," said Jones, "I think that the crew and some others are gathered in the crew quarters. What they are doing in there, I do not know."

"It would be foolish to walk right in there," added Nasir.

"Let's try a little distraction and see what happens. I will go across to the truck and start the engine. It should attract some attention, and then you can take a look in the crew quarters while all eyes are focused in my direction," suggested Jones. "Get in position and wait until you hear the engine start up." He headed away in the same direction as his previous scouting trip.

Nasir quietly approached the crew quarters and hid himself in a hollow quite close to the tent. Jones got into the cab of the truck and started it up. He revved the engine to make as much noise as possible, and then he sunk low behind the driver's seat.

A figure immediately rushed out of the crew's quarters and headed straight for the truck. Seeing no one, the man circled the vehicle slowly. He found nothing and saw no one. He finally stopped and stood with uncertainty near the cab door. The truck's engine was still running, so the man gathered his courage and moved to open the door of the cab. As he reached into the cab to turn off the engine, Jones's fist clubbed him to the ground.

At the same time, Nasir crawled around to the tent opening. Seeing no immediate danger, he stood up and walked into the tent to find four crew members tied up and lying on their cots.

"Look out!" called the director, but his warning came too late. Nasir was seized from behind by a burly Arab.

"Now, what have we here?" said the Arab. "What a puny little man you are. Keep still or I will break your neck." Nasir could hardly breathe in his tight grip.

"Where are your allies?" he asked. "Come with me, my little friend." He lifted Nasir out of the tent and carried him to the center of the camp.

"Wherever you are," called the Arab, "Come! Stand where I can see you. I have your friend here. I will not harm him, if you come out now."

"Snap!" said Jones, revolver in hand, as he stepped into the open using his victim as a shield.

"Throw down your weapon," said the Arab, "and you will come to no harm."

"Throw down your weapon, and you will come to no harm," mimicked Jones.

"If you do not surrender, I will be forced to give you a demonstration of my intent," said the Arab.

"If you do not surrender, I ... I may be forced to do likewise."

The Arab fired his pistol into the air. Jones fired his revolver in a similar fashion.

"I have warned you for the last time," said the Arab. He pointed his pistol at Nasir's foot and fired. Nasir screamed with pain, but the burly Arab did not loosen his grip.

"Enough of this horseplay," said Jones. Without hesitation he put a bullet through the opposing Arab's kneecap. The Arab fell to the ground writhing in agony, his weapon falling away. Nasir also hit the ground. A small trickle of blood showed through his boot. Jones released his captive and directed him to sit on the ground, where he secured him with some twine..

Nasir, despite his pain, picked up the Arab's pistol. "Shall I finish him off?" he enquired.

"He's no problem now," said Jones. "Let me see that foot of yours."

The Arab's pistol shot had neatly removed Nasir's little toe. It was a clean wound.

Jones completely disregarded the big Arab, who was writhing and cursing on the ground. Instead he focused on assisting Nasir to his own tent, where he located his first aid kit, cleansed the wound, and sowed up the gap left by the missing toe.

"Can you walk?" enquired Jones.

Nasir stood up and, despite the pain, appeared to walk quite freely. "There is little pain. I think I can manage," he said. They returned to check on the Arab and his colleague and then went on to the crew's quarters, where they freed the crew and the director.

"So what on earth has been going on here today?" asked Jones.

5

I t had been early afternoon when the crew and the director were taking their rest and the tourists were out scouting the area, that a couple of men mounted on camels made a quiet approach to the campsite. Noticing them drawing near, the director emerged from his tent and came forward to address them.

"Greetings my friends," said the director. "What is your business at my campsite?"

The pair remained mounted. The larger of the two spoke. "We understand that you have a tourist here by the name of Norman. We have business with him."

"Mr. Norman is out investigating the area at the moment. He will return at sunset," said the director. "You are welcome to wait here for his arrival."

The pair slid from their camels and allowed them to kneel in the rest position. The visitors then approached the director to make their introductions. The director spoke first.

"I am the director of the In the Footsteps of Moses Tour. And you are?"

"I am El Gasim, and you will do exactly as I say." responded the man, who now appeared to be much larger and more hostile as he drew a pistol from within his robes.

The director pleaded, "Please don't do anything foolish."

"How many men do you have working here?"

"There are three men resting in the tent over there," responded the director.

"Call your head man to come out," instructed El Gasim.

The director responded immediately. "Joash! Joash, come out here this minute!" After a few moments, Joash wandered sleepily out of the tent.

"What is it?" he asked, unaware of the danger.

"This is a pistol," said El Gasim quietly. "Do as you are told, and you won't get hurt. Hands behind your back." The director and Joash were bound with their hands tied behind them, then they were forced to walk in front of the hostile pair to the tent door. "Wake up, my friends. Wake up, my prisoners," called El Gasim as they entered the tent. The remaining crew was soon tied up, and all four were secured to their beds. "You will all wait quietly for the return of Mr. Norman, while we find out what your tourists have to eat."

And so it was when Jones and Nasir came upon the quiet campsite. The criminals sat waiting in silence, watching over their prisoners.

6

"What shall we do with this villain?" queried Jones.
"We don't want him here," responded the director, "but I think that you should see what you can do to fix his wound."

Jones came upon the still cursing Gasim. "Keep still, and I will see how I can help you." said Jones to the angry man. He cleaned up the wound as best he could. "It is no use," Jones told the director. "This man needs to be taken to a hospital. He needs proper medical care."

"The nearest hospital is in Jeddan, which is well beyond where our route turns inland," responded the director.

"Nasir and I could take him there, if you like," Jones volunteered. "We could look around that area at the same time."

"Well, if you insist, that would suit me and the tourists," said the director. "We break camp tomorrow morning and turn inland. I can supply you with the relevant maps, so that you can find us again."

"What about our other friend here?" said Jones indicating Gasim's companion.

"We can keep him here overnight and then release him when we leave in the morning. The long walk to the nearest village will do him good," said the director. "You will unfortunately miss out on tonight's special meal, but we will prepare food and water for you to take with you on your journey."

Jones and Nasir made quick preparations to leave. Strapping Gasim firmly to his camel and taking the other camel as a spare, they set off for Jeddan. After an hour, they joined a well-defined track that Nasir knew would take them to their destination. He led the way, with the camel carrying Gasim tied in behind. Then Jones followed with the spare camel in tow. The procession made good progress, but it was early evening when they finally rode into Jeddan.

They first found the police outpost, where local police were delighted to see Gasim or "El Gasim" as he was known to them. Their delight was short-lived when Jones insisted that Gasim be delivered to the area hospital. When he pointed out Gasim's wound and therefore inability to escape, the police became more willing to release him into the care of medical authorities.

Jones, Nasir, and Gasim, accompanied by a police officer, made the short trip to the hospital. Gasim was given immediate attention by the medical staff. Then Jones insisted that Nasir have his toe examined by an intern.

"It appears to be a clean amputation," said the intern. "I will put in a fresh suture and give the foot a clean dressing, but otherwise time alone will heal the wound."

Gasim was also receiving proper treatment, so Jones felt that they could leave in good conscience. As the two men emerged from the hospital, Nasir said, "I have an uncle here in Jeddan. We could stay overnight with him."

"Excellent!" responded Jones. "I could use some rest. It's

been a long day." They found the four camels, their own and the two belonging to the criminals, which Nasir appeared determined to keep. Nasir lead the way through a variety of alleyways until they arrived in a wide square. They approached a compound, only to be met by furiously barking dogs. A voice from inside the building yelled a command, and they suddenly became quiet.

"Who comes in the night uninvited?"

"Your lowly nephew and his friend seek hospitality this night," responded Nasir.

"Nasir! Is it you? Nasir ben Loham?"

"Yes, it is I, Nasir ben Loham, nephew of Joachim ben Loham."

Joachim emerged from the shadows and spoke. "Welcome to you, and shalom! Welcome to your friend. Please, please come this way."

They were ushered into the building, where a late family meal was just being cleared away. They were given a place to sit, and then food was provided for them. Coffee was brought in, and soon Joachim led the conversation.

"What is it that brings you so far from home, Nasir?"

Nasir related the incident at the campsite and their need to bring Gasim to Jeddan.

"So, El Gasim has been brought down to Earth at last," commented Joachim. "And you, Major Jones, what is it that brings you to our area?"

"I am on a tour of the Red Sea area, following in Moses' footsteps, so to speak," Jones replied. "I am an archaeologist, and Nasir is helping me with my research."

"He is most interested in the brass serpents that many of our villages display," added Nasir.

"Have you shown him your village emblem?" asked Joachim.

"Yes, we have been there and seen that," said Jones.

"What about the old Hebrew village northeast of here?" asked Joachim.

"I had forgotten all about that," said Nasir. "It is possible that we could stop there on our return journey tomorrow."

"As it happens, our family has a miniature copy of the serpent," interposed Joachim. "There was a time when many families owned their own copy, but that time has long past. Would you like to see our copy?"

"Yes, please!" responded Jones. "It would be a rare treat to see such a thing close up."

"Well, come and see it for yourself. It's over here in this case." Jones followed Joachim to a glass case in the corner of the room, not unlike the case that contained the snake he had viewed previously that day. Joachim opened the container and lifted out a miniature of the serpent on a pole. He thrust the object into Jones's hands in a most casual way. Clearly, this item had no value in Joachim's opinion. The miniature was a blend of wood and metal. It was highly polished and clearly made by a master craftsman. Jones was instantly seized by its beauty. The serpent had a hidden quality that perhaps was hidden from Joachim's eye.

"Come over here to the light," indicated Joachim.

Jones peered at the serpent for quite some time, murmuring to himself about its unusual qualities.

"You like it?" questioned Joachim.

"Yes, my own family would be delighted to have an artifact like this. It has deep meaning for us. An item like this would be treasured."

"Would you like to buy it?" asked Joachim.

"I can't believe that you would actually part with this. How much do you want for it?" queried Jones.

"Two hundred American dollars would be a fair price," responded Joachim.

"This is not the time for doing business, my uncle," interposed Nasir. "Can you not see how tired Major Jones has become? Let us retire to the comfort of a bed, and then perhaps tomorrow you can talk of a price."

Jones was taken aback by Nasir's intervention, but he did feel strangely tired and made no protest as they were ushered into a small room. As Jones prepared for bed, Nasir excused himself, saying that he needed to catch up on family news and happenings in Jeddan. Jones made no complaint. He lay down on the bed, leaving aside his normal ritual, and fell asleep.

7

He awoke to bright sunlight, much to his consternation. "Nasir?" he called softly.

"Don't worry, Major Jones," responded Nasir. "We, in this family, are what you would call late sleepers."

They arose and prepared themselves for the day. Some members of the family had also stirred, and after a light breakfast, Jones and Nasir were sent away with fresh supplies of food and water.

Jones and Nasir lead their camels for quite a distance, until it was clear that the road ahead would allow them to mount. They rode on quietly, Jones trusting that Nasir had already determined their route to the tour's new campsite.

"We are two camels short!" announced Jones, suddenly realizing that two of the four camels were missing.

"On the other hand," responded Nasir, "what is it that my uncle has placed among your food supplies?"

Jones reached forward to the bag slung over his camel's saddle. He felt inside and, to his amazement, found the miniature wrapped in some rags. "How on earth did you manage that?"

"My uncle has many such things for sale," smiled Nasir. "It was only a matter of finding the right price. It was a fair swap."

"I really am indebted to you, Nasir," said Jones. He began to wonder how he could fully repay Nasir for his kindness. This was no ordinary family that he was dealing with.

As intended, Nasir eventually found the trail that headed toward the old Hebrew village. It was much further than they thought, and it was noon before they found the derelict site.

"Not much of a tourist attraction," commented Jones. "Nothing much to see here at all."

"We can at least view the village emblem," said Nasir.

He rode on toward the spot where the village emblem stood. The pole was there, but nothing could be seen of the emblem.

"Somebody has removed it," commented Jones.

"We can find out from Arba, the village keeper," responded Nasir. "He is watching us from a dwelling somewhere around here, so I've been instructed."

They quietly toured the scattered ramshackle houses of the old village, until suddenly they were challenged in Arabic by a loud voice. "What is it that you seek? State your business!"

"We come seeking understanding," responded Nasir in a very pompous voice.

"Who is it that seeks understanding? Give me your name and family."

"I am Nasir ben Loham. My father is Loham ben Loham, a man of renown."

"Loham, eh? Then welcome Nasir ben Loham," said a

small, sharp featured man who emerged from one of the buildings. "And who do you bring with you? Not another thieving tourist?"

"No tourist, sir," responded Jones in Arabic, "but one who seeks the reason."

"Major Jones, meet Arba, keeper of the village. Arba, meet Major Jones, a man with many questions," said Nasir.

"Welcome, Major Jones. Shalom! Welcome to a man who understands our tongue. Now, what questions do you have?" enquired Arba, as the pair dismounted.

"Why is it that many villages have their emblem on display, but here it has been removed?"

Arba ushered them inside his small shack, which was pleasantly furnished despite its outward derelict appearance. "Our village emblem has been missing for decades," said Arba, continuing the conversation. "Many people seek its power. Many have died protecting it."

"Why would people seek a copy of the brass serpent?" asked Jones. "It would have no real value."

"Value? Value?" shouted Arba. "Who can put a price on healing? Our emblem is not what many thought it to be. It is no copy. It is the original brass serpent used by the Hebrew Moses."

"You say 'is.' It *is* the original brass serpent? Do you really mean that it still exists?" Jones asked in disbelief.

"Since you come as a friend of Nasir ben Loham," said Arba, "I can assure you that the brass serpent still exists. It was hidden for centuries where no one would expect to find it—on top of our village pole. However, the enemy was searching for it and moving closer. So in the end, for its own safety, it was removed to a safer place."

"I understood from reading the Old Testament that the brass serpent was taken by the Hebrews on their journey to the Promised Land. It became a sort of religious icon for the people. I am very interested in its healing power," Jones added.

"The whole world is still seeking the healing power of the brass serpent," said Arba, "so you are right to be interested in it. However, there is only one place the power is effective, and that is in this area. It can still be used against snakes, but only those of this region."

"I didn't know that there were any snakes in this area," challenged Jones, "At least not in the significant numbers of Moses's time."

"We have many snakes in this area, but they are the two-legged kind," said Arba.

"As it happens, I have recently purchased a miniature copy of the brass serpent," said Jones. "Would you like to see it?" Reaching for his satchel, Jones brought out the miniature. "Is this anything like the original?" he asked.

Arba took the brass serpent carefully into his hands. He looked intently into its eyes and examined the area surrounding the throat. "Yes! It has a remarkable likeness to the real brass serpent."

Suddenly there was a loud cry from outside the shack.

"Arba! Arba, come quickly! Hasan has been wounded!"

The three rushed outside to find a young man mounted on his camel. "There have been more intruders near our home," he continued. "Hasan has been badly hurt. You must come. He needs your help."

"I must leave you," said Arba. "Perhaps I will see you another time?"

"If we come with you," said Jones, "I may be able to help.

I have skill as a surgeon." Arba nodded his assent and scurried back into the shack. The two picked up their gear and hastened back to the waiting Arba, who was mounted on the camel behind the young man. Wheeling their camels around, they set off at a strong pace, and within fifteen minutes they arrived at Arba's home.

The customary greetings were omitted in the heat of tending to the stricken Hasan, who was found lying on the floor, tended to by his mother and her daughter.

"He is fading," the mother said. "There has been great loss of blood."

"Let me see the wound," said Jones in a commanding voice. Arba nodded his approval, and Hasan's mother moved to one side. Jones put his extensive medical experience gained in the Royal Army Medical Corps to immediate use and diagnosed the shoulder wound. "Has the bullet been removed?" he asked.

"No bullet."

"I need something clean to probe the wound, and I need it now," said Jones as he applied pressure to the wound. The family searched quickly for an appropriate instrument. "I need hot water, too, and some bandages."

A small kitchen implement was found and brought to the scene.

"Alcohol. Have you any alcohol?" demanded Jones.

A bottle of spirits was brought out, and the family looked on in amazement as Jones washed his hands and the implement with it. Jones then used the tool to probe carefully into the wound. Hasan groaned quietly. As the probing went more deeply into the wound, Hasan's groaning intensified. Jones, working as quickly as he could, finally found the bullet, which was lodged deep in the shoulder muscle. Using the probe and his fingers, he drew out the bullet and then promptly poured into the wound a large quantity of the alcohol. He then drew the flesh together and cleaned the wound as best he could. It was bound up and the shoulder immobilized.

Jones made Hasan as comfortable as possible, and then he turned to the family and said, "If you have a God, then now would be a good time to pray to him on behalf of Hasan."

"We pray to the same god that the Hebrews worshipped," responded Arba. The family fell silent as they watched over Hasan. At the same time they offered up their prayers. After what seemed an eternity, Hasan appeared to breathe in a more peaceful fashion. Jones moved out of the room to get some fresh air and also give the family time to voice their prayers.

"Will he live?" asked Nasir.

"I think we got here just in time," said Jones.

Arba joined them a few moments later. "Hasan sleeps. All is well."

"Praise God," Jones sighed.

"Come, let us take some refreshments, my friends," said Arba.

8

Arba led them to an adjacent room where coffee was served with various delicacies. They relaxed and chatted informally until Arba brought the conversation back to Jones's research.

"Major Jones, I have something to show you." Nasir looked apprehensively at Arba, uncertain of what was to follow. "I have observed your skill as a surgeon today, and I feel that my family is indebted to you." He paused a moment and then resumed. "You have expressed a real interest in the brass serpent, as you call it. Well, you will be surprised to learn that it is here."

Jones stuttered, "H-h-here?"

"Yes, here!" said Arba. "I feel that I can let you see it."

"That would be absolutely wonderful!" exclaimed Jones. "Do we have far to travel to see it?"

"No distance at all," responded Arba. "It is here! It is here in my home, where my family has protected it for many years." Arba led the way down a narrow passage. Pausing to unlatch a door he said, "Be careful as you make your way down these steps. We have not placed any lights here." Jones and the others groped their way slowly down the stairs that led toward a dimly lit room.

"It's all right, Abar!" called Arba. "We have a guest with us." A tall youth emerged from the shadows near the door. Abar carried an automatic rifle on his shoulder, and he moved aside to allow the group to enter the poorly lit room. A single light played directly on a large, covered display cabinet in the center of the room.

"Are you ready, Major Jones, for the sight of your life?" challenged Arba, who swept aside the cover to reveal the brass serpent. "Behold, Nehushtan!" Jones gasped at what he saw, for it was not the glorious sight that he had expected. "We have tidied it up a little since its time on the village pole."

"Not at all impressive," thought Jones to himself. "I wonder why there is such a desire to have this miserable-looking object. Why would people kill for such a thing?"

"Bring up the lights," called Arba to Abar. "Now, Major Jones, if you will focus your full attention on the head of Nehushtan, you may see something quite astonishing."

As the light increased, the serpent appeared to come alive. There was a mysterious glowing around its jaws. Its eyes became bright and shone with a strange luminescence. Jones was transfixed as a hidden force grasped him and held him in a trance. His body tingled with excitement, for he beheld a sight that was too profound, too unearthly, too intoxicating to comprehend. He continued to stare, entranced by the supernatural vision. After a period of time, the light was diminished at Arba's signal.

"I think you have seen enough for one day, Major Jones."

Jones gradually emerged from his trance and followed Arba meekly up the stairs. Still enchanted, he stammered his thanks.

"Now you can see why we protect Nehushtan from outsiders," said Arba. "We will, of course, expect you to tell no one of your experience this day."

"Of course, of course," mumbled Jones. Then recovering a bit he added, "You say that the healing power only works on those bitten by snakes from this area?"

"That is correct," said Arba. "That was the purpose for which Nehushtan was made by Moses."

"Nehushtan, as you call it, does seem to have strange powers that may have nothing to do with snakes," said Jones.

"We are aware of that," Arba responded, "but what these powers are for and who they are to help we do not know. Nonetheless, we protect Nehushtan from anyone who may want to misuse its power."

"Very wise," agreed Jones. "This name, Nehushtan, where does it come from?"

"I am indeed surprised that in your research you have not seen the name before," said Arba. "You will find it in the Jewish Holy Book, in the section called Kings. People worshipped Nehushtan at that time and sought its powers."

"I don't remember reading about that," confessed Jones.

"The Hebrew Bible tells that Nehushtan was destroyed, but we, the keepers of Nehushtan, know that only one of the two brass serpents made by Moses was destroyed. Moses was wise enough to recognize that Nehushtan's power would be most needed here in this area. We believe that he left the people of this region a copy for themselves. After all, this is the place where the need first arose."

"Absolutely wonderful!" responded Jones. "I must look up this word Nehushtan when I get home."

Their conversation returned to their joint concern over Hasan. "We will need to move Hasan to a hospital," Jones warned.

"We will see to that at the right time," responded Arba. "Now let us get you on your way, following in the footsteps of Moses."

After consulting Jones's map, Nasir and Arba decided how best to reach the tour's next campsite. "I will send Abar with you as your guide and protector," said Arba, "for this is not a safe place for anyone these days."

The trio set off in a northeasterly direction, with Abar leading the way. They soon came across an ancient trail heading in the right direction. He halted and instructed his traveling companions. "I will wait and rest here for awhile, just to make sure that we have not been followed," said Abar. "The way from here is well marked." He drew aside as Jones and Nasir continued on the track. "May your god go with you and prosper your way."

Nasir responded, "God defend you and your family."

Jones and Nasir continued onward, even though it was well past noon and the sun's rays had begun to penetrate their light covering. "Could be another two hours to the campsite," said Nasir. "If we press on, we could meet up with them before dark."

9

The two hours dragged by slowly, as they pushed their camels gently forward. Finally, they saw the sun's rays reflecting on shiny surfaces in the distance. As they drew closer, they observed a thin column of smoke rising into the air; the crew was already preparing dinner. Jones and Nasir both heaved sighs of relief, as the camp activity appeared normal. They rode slowly into the site, where the director was bustling around as usual.

"Ah, Major Jones and Nasir! Glad to see you made it back before nightfall," he said. "We are nearly all gathered for dinner. We are just awaiting Mr. Norman and Mr. Elder, who have not yet returned from today's exploration. At sunset we shall dine, whether or not they are here."

Jones found his way to his tent with his precious cargo and discussed with Nasir how best to protect it. "How on earth can I keep this safe?" he asked.

"If you like, I could stay with the tour as your assistant," proposed Nasir. "I could watch over your belongings, be your guide, and as you English say, "watch your back."

"Excellent!" responded Jones. "Yes, I would appreciate that."

After they had a chance to freshen up, Jones and Nasir joined the tourists at the dining area, which was set up and ready for the meal.

The director was agitated. "It's no use waiting any longer," he sputtered. "We will just have to go ahead and eat." He indicated to the crew that they should begin to serve drinks and uncover the food. All present filled their plates. Some of the men ate as if it were their last meal on earth. Eventually, when all were satisfied, they relaxed.

As the last drink was being served, conversation started up, focusing on the absence of Norman and Elder. Well before noon, the tour had arrived at the present site, and, after a short rest, Norman and Elder moved out to explore the immediate area. The pair was thought to be no more than a mile from the camp, so why hadn't they returned? As night fell, the party of tourists became more and more concerned over the fate of Norman and Elder. The director was going out of his mind with worry.

Suddenly, there was a distant shout. "Help me! Someone, please, come and help me!" It was Elder.

The director rushed out of the camp toward the general direction of his cry. "Over here," he called. The crew ran after him. Within about forty meters, they came upon Elder, who was half-dragging, half-carrying Norman. The crew picked up the injured man and carried him to his tent. At the same time, the director assisted Elder back to the camp. After gulping down a cold, refreshing drink, Elder pulled himself together and recounted the events of the day.

"We were about two miles from here, on our way back to

the camp, when Norman saw what looked like an interesting marked stone." Jones glanced meaningfully at Nasir, as Elder continued. "We took notes on the engraving, and while I dusted off the stone, Norman found a small cavity underneath it. He put his hand into the cavity, fished around inside, and found one or two interesting pieces. Then again he reached inside the cavity. He suddenly cried out in pain, when he thought that he might have been nipped by something. There were no marks on his hand, so we thought nothing more of it at the time.

"We completed our survey of the site and moved on. As we were walking back, he complained of feeling unwell. Then, he developed a headache. We kept going until he passed out. For the last half hour I have been carrying him."

The director stepped in. "Then it may well be a snake bite. I'll get the serum." He was back in a trice with the medical kit.

"Let me see that!" commanded Jones. He took the container from the director and scanned its contents. "Is this all you have?"

"This is all I have ever needed," said the director.

"Better give the serum a try then," suggested Jones. They went immediately to Norman's tent, and a dose of serum was injected. "I'll keep watch for a while," said Jones.

After an hour, there were some signs of recovery. "We need to keep a close watch over him," said Jones to the director.

"I'll have one of the crew stay with him," he responded.

The remaining tourists wandered off to bed, now that the excitement was over.

Around midnight, the director roused Jones with news that Norman had become delirious. "What shall I do now?" he asked.

"Give him another shot of the serum," said Jones from his bed. "Call me if that doesn't do the trick." The director bustled away again, leaving Jones to sleep.

It appeared to be no time at all before the director was back again rousing Jones. "Major Jones! Major Jones! It's starting to look very bad for Norman. Please come! We need your help now!" Jones awoke instantly. He arose from his bed and followed the director to Norman's cot. "He has had three doses of serum. One dose is usually enough," said the director. "I haven't seen anything like this before."

"Oh, I've seen it before," said Jones, remembering his own wife's close call with death. "You need to face it, this could be fatal."

Norman was delirious and sweating profusely. The pair worked to cool him down with damp towels, but apart from that, there was little else they could do.

"I wish that there was something else that we could try," moaned the director.

"There is one thing that we might try," said Jones in a guarded tone.

"Anything! Anything is better than nothing," responded the director.

"Just wait here," said Jones, who went off in search of Nasir.

"Nasir," he whispered, "we have a problem."

Nasir was awake in a flash. "What is it?"

"Norman is in a bad way. I need to try something to help him. Will you assist me?"

"Of course. Anything," he responded.

"Get the miniature and bring it to Norman's tent."

Nasir rose and carried out Jones instructions, keeping

the miniature covered as he carried it across the campsite. At Norman's bedside, the three conferred together.

"First, we need to wake Norman up," said Jones. "And I mean really wake him."

"We have some ice," said the director. "If we apply it to his neck and head, he may come around briefly." As the ice was being sought, Jones explained to Nasir what he intended to do.

An extra lamp was brought to the tent, and the miniature was carefully unveiled. The director brought in the ice, along with a basin of water.

"Just leave this to us for now," said Jones to the director. "You go and rest for awhile." The director must have been quite tired, for he willingly submitted to the request, not realizing that Jones wanted him out of the way.

Once alone, the pair got on with the task of saving Norman's life. Together they applied the ice and cold water to his neck and head. He became very quiet for a moment as the ice broke the fever's hold. Then Jones began to shake the patient.

"Norman! Norman! Wake up, man." He did this several times, and eventually a groggy Norman responded.

"What! What?"

"Look at the snake," Jones commanded.

Norman's eyes closed again. Nasir held both lamps, so that the serpent's head was fully illuminated.

"Closer!" Jones demanded. Then to Norman he said, "Look at the snake. Look at the snake. Concentrate on the snake!" Norman must have given the snake the faintest of glances, for suddenly his eyes opened wide, and he was able to focus on the serpent. He took in the vision fully for a brief moment, and then he fell slowly back into oblivion. The conflict was over, although only time would tell who had won the battle.

10

As dawn slowly broke over the camp, Jones carried out another check of the patient's condition. There was no longer any fever, but Norman lay very still, hardly breathing. Life was still in him, but just barely.

The crew began their early morning preparations for breakfast. The tourists also started their morning dance, as one by one they occupied the shower area and the latrine.

Nasir emerged from the crew quarters and went across to Norman's tent to relieve Jones of his responsibility. They acknowledged each other briefly, and then Jones took his turn for some much-needed sleep.

He lay on his bed, turning over the events of the past few days. He did not keep a strict diary, as many archaeologists did. The events of the last three days had been so demanding that taking time to complete his scant notes had not been a priority. Oh, how he wished that he had made some brief notes instead of being left to the confused memories that were circling in his mind.

The dream, the writing on the stone, the vision of the brass serpent, and this recent crisis all seemed to fit into some huge puzzle. If only he could see the overall picture, then it would all make sense. In this confused state, he fell asleep.

After breakfast, the director resumed his normal briefing routine, directing the tourists to stay together, carry a weapon, and let him know exactly where they would be exploring. He refrained from telling them not to put their hands into rock cavities, assuming that the lesson had been learned. The maps were issued; food and water were supplied. The remaining four tourists broke into twos and went their way. The crew got on with their daily chores, and in a short while, the camp fell silent.

The director met up with Elder in his quarters. "Now, Mr. Elder," he began, "I want to express my concern over yesterday's events. I have for you, and especially for Mr. Norman, a few questions that need answering concerning the men who visited our camp."

"I have a couple of questions, too," added Jones, who appeared at the tent entrance. His turbulent thoughts had not allowed him to sleep for long.

"There is nothing really to tell," said Elder. "Norman purchased some items from an Arab last season in Jeddan. He and the fellow named Gasim had something going on between them that needed sorting out."

"What kind of items are we talking about?" asked Jones.

"Nothing of much value, I assure you," said Elder.

"What exactly is your interest in this region?" asked the director.

"We collect mainly Hebrew artifacts," said Elder, "things that were dropped or left behind by the Hebrews when they passed through here three thousand years ago. We pick up bits and pieces here and there, wherever we find them. These are taken back to the States, where we sell them to various universities for a small profit. We are not in it for the money, if that is what you are thinking."

"Well, we have one man in hospital; Nasir has lost a toe; and Mr. Norman over there is at death's door," said the director. "So I do hope that you are happy with the 'small profit' you have made. You can't tell me that there isn't something gravely wrong with what you two are doing."

"You'll have to ask Norman about it yourself then," said Elder, defending himself.

"Oh, we will," responded Jones.

The director and Jones exchanged meaningful glances and then left Elder to his own devices. Jones returned to check on a sleeping Norman, who appeared to be breathing slightly more deeply. Jones yawned loudly, reminding himself of his need for more sleep. He went back to his tent and fell immediately asleep.

The sun was high in the sky, when Nasir roused Jones from his slumber. "Norman is waking," he said. Jones reluctantly arose from his bed and followed Nasir across the campsite to Norman's tent. Jones quickly checked Norman's vital signs.

"He is looking a lot better," said Jones. "Norman will need some water as soon as he comes around."

Nasir went out to fetch a water container, and when he returned he found that Norman had indeed woken up. He raised Norman's shoulders up so that he could drink. "Drink this," he said. "Slowly! Slowly!" After awhile, he let Norman sink back onto his bed.

"You look a lot better now than you did last night," said Jones. "You've had a close call. How do you feel now?"

"I feel that I have experienced one horrendous nightmare," began Norman.

"What can you remember of the last few days?" asked Jones.

"I remember being bitten by something, and I remember trying to walk with Elder." Norman continued. "Then everything went black. I remember being here on this bed, sweating like mad. Then I remember that I had an awful dream; there was this massive snake trying to eat me, and it had hypnotic eyes and nearly frightened me to death."

"Well, you did come close to death," Jones informed the man. "You suffered from a bad case of snakebite, but you pulled through. So I think you should rest up for the remainder of the day."

"I feel that I could sleep for ever," responded Norman.

"He nearly did," commented Nasir to Jones.

Jones and Nasir withdrew from Norman's tent, leaving him to rest.

Seeing that the director was free, Jones went to speak to him. "Norman has recovered," he began. "What do you think that he did to Gasim to make him so angry?"

"There is a lot of illegal trading going on in the whole of Arabia. It could be that Norman got more than a bargain at some point from Gasim, and he later realized it. Gasim is not the sort that you should try to cheat."

"Rather bad tempered," added Jones.

"Anyway, this will put an end to Norman's trading in this area, and of course Gasim will be much easier to catch now, if you get my meaning." the director grinned.

"Norman is resting today, but I think that he will be well

enough to travel tomorrow." Jones paused and then began a new avenue of discussion. "What area exactly were Norman and Elder working in yesterday?"

"I'll show you on today's map," said the director.

They crossed to the office, where the director indicated the area of interest on a map.

"We could take a look at that region ourselves. We might find the place where Norman received his bite. There might be something worth noting there," said Jones.

"You have four hours of sunlight left. Don't get lost, and," the director paused for effect, "don't put your hand into any holes." Jones appreciated the humor, which helped break the ice in their formal relationship.

He summoned Nasir and told him of his plans to explore the site. They gathered the customary essentials, including weapons, for their trip, even though the distance was not great. "Better to be safe than sorry, eh Nasir?" Jones said.

Nasir had been surprised and delighted to hear of the site Norman and Elder appeared to have uncovered. It would be something new to show future tourists. They mounted their camels and headed in the direction indicated by the director. When they had covered two miles, there was still no sign of a stone monument or whatever it was. They stopped and worked out their position on the map.

"Looks like there is a mound or hill of some sort to the

south. Can you see it?" Nasir glimpsed something odd and added, "Let's look over there." They moved slowly in a southerly direction and soon came upon a rough mound.

"This looks man-made," said Jones. "No wonder it isn't on the map."

"And here is your pile of stones," indicated Nasir, spotting a roughly cemented rock pile halfway up the mound.

They dismounted from the camels and carefully picked their way up the side of the hill, which was not more than twenty feet high.

"Not at all easy to find," commented Jones. "Tread carefully, and watch where you put your hands."

The monument was more or less as Elder had described it, except for the mound, which was of more interest to Jones than Elder could have imagined. As they moved up and around the focal point, their feet kept slipping. "This was put up in haste," Jones noted to himself. There was a larger stone, which was surrounded and cemented to the other stones. It bore a long inscription. Jones copied the writing carefully into his notebook, then spoke meaningfully for Nasir's benefit.

"Nasir," he said, "this is very important for you. Listen to this." He paused, then began to translate carefully, "Here lies the family of Loham. For them Nehushtan came too late."

"Would you repeat that?" said Nasir, not quite grasping the significance of what he heard and saw.

"Here lies the family of Loham. For them Nehushtan came too late," repeated Jones. There was silence as they both drank in the importance of the inscription. Jones spoke first. "This is the first time I have come across the word Nehushtan in any form of ancient writing. I think that we have found a very special site."

"It is even more special to me and to my family," said Nasir. "This confirms that we, a family of Loham, are indeed descended from the Hebrews. It confirms that we really do belong to this area."

"More than that, Nasir," said Jones. "Your ancestors may lie under this mound. This could even be a mass grave."

"This is not a memorial, it's a disaster. Who could have done such a thing?"

"They were buried in haste, I would say." said Jones. "No time for any ceremony. Family ties being what they were, someone may have actually volunteered to stay behind and tend the graves. Perhaps someone who really loved those who died decided to stay behind and keep watch, someone named Loham."

"Well someone, a descendant, took the time to write an inscription and set it in the middle of the mound," said Nasir.

"From the position of our campsite, I would say that there may have been water in this region few centuries ago. The area could have been a lot more hospitable then."

"This is a real mystery," said Nasir. "I will have to tell my father of this find. He will want to come here and see for himself."

"While we are here, let's find that hollow that Norman put his hand into," said Jones. They carefully scoured the region around the inscription. Much of the stone appeared to be just sitting on the surface. The dirt was very loose. The whole mound had a feeling of impermanence. Reexamining the inscription, Jones brought out a small brush from his satchel and dusted carefully the area surrounding the inscription. There was no indication of any drawings of a snake.

"So, that's that," said Jones. "Nothing else for me here."

"Perhaps not for you," said Nasir, "but for me there lies ahead a lifelong task." He paused a moment, and then added, "If you don't mind, I ask you never to disclose to anyone the things that we have found today."

"Of course, of course, my friend," said Jones. "We have a few secrets in common now, have we not? We need to keep them in the family."

They tidied up the top of the mound as best they could, then they slid back down the slope. As they turned to walk to where the camels waited, Jones stopped Nasir and pointed to a rough track leaving the base of the mound.

"I hadn't noticed before, but there appears to be a path leading from here and curving around the next little mound over there." He pointed toward the east. "We have time. Let's take a look." Sure enough, as they followed the winding path, it began to widen and became more substantial.

"Someone has been using this track for quite some time," confirmed Nasir.

"It must lead somewhere," added Jones. They followed the track, which appeared to be endless, winding around and around various mounds.

"What about our camels?" queried Jones. "They won't wander off, will they?"

"Let's keep going for a few more minutes," insisted Nasir.

They pressed on, and Jones became more apprehensive with each passing moment. The track widened suddenly into an open, flat space. A few stones were scattered here and there showing the outline a small building.

"Looks like the remains of a dwelling of some sort," said Jones.

They looked around the area and found that many other stones were lying half buried in the ground. The stones had been deliberately scattered in all directions, as if the building had been destroyed in anger. They came upon a freshly disturbed piece of ground to the rear of the area.

"Not much of a garden," quipped Jones.

"This is not a garden, my friend," said Nasir. "This is a grave." They paused at the site, differing thoughts welling up within them.

"Perhaps this is the grave of the person who tended the mound?" asked Jones.

"Then, I wonder who dug the grave," said Nasir. "I will have to investigate this further."

"Well, I'm getting hungry, and I'm not going one more step today."

"Don't worry, I will have plenty of time to follow up," said Nasir. "Just wait until I tell my father of our findings today. He will be really intrigued." Nasir turned to find that Jones was already heading back along the track. He gave up his quest until a more appropriate day.

They found their camels and returned to the camp, which was bustling with activity as the crew began to set out the evening meal. Nasir and Jones rode quietly to the perimeter of the site and "parked" the camels. They headed to Norman's tent first to check on the patient.

"How are you, Norman?" asked Jones, as they entered the tent.

Norman responded brightly, "Quite good, considering."

"Considering that you nearly died last night," added Elder, who was seated at his side.

"Well, I could eat a horse now," said Norman.

"You might have something there," said Elder. "We haven't found out what we are having for dinner yet, but there is a very unusual smell in the air."

"That would be the camels," said Nasir.

The director came in just then to check up on Norman's condition. "All's well then?"

"As well as can be expected," said Norman in hostile tone.

"We will reach Akaba in four days. Then the tour will be complete," said the director. "Can you keep up the pace until then?"

"I'll manage somehow," growled Norman.

"And you, Major Jones, have you found the tour beneficial?"

"It has been most illuminating," said Jones in a noncommittal tone, not wanting to show any excitement over his recent findings. "Any news from back home? I have been out of touch for these last few days."

"Cricket at Manchester was rained off as usual. Northern Ireland has troubles," said the director. "The Royal Family has all the usual things going on. Oh! One thing. In the northeast of England some miners have been dying of a mystery illness. Apart from that, nothing much."

"I see," said Jones. "So, as usual, nothing new in the news. Well, I had better get on with a bit of writing. There is so much to catch up on with my research and travels during these last few days."

Jones and Nasir left the tent and retired to Jones's quarters, where they discussed their future plans. Jones indicated that he would be leaving Arabia and returning to England and to his family. Perhaps he would plan a return trip next year. Time would tell. On the other hand, Nasir was filled with inspiration over the recent find. He was bursting to tell his family his news.

Jones checked Nasir's foot to see if there was any sign of infection. The wound was healing nicely. However, Jones gave his new-found friend all the extra cash that he had on hand to meet any future medical expenses, should they arise.

A few days later, they parted company at Akaba with their friendship truly cemented. They looked forward to renewing their acquaintance during the next tourist season.

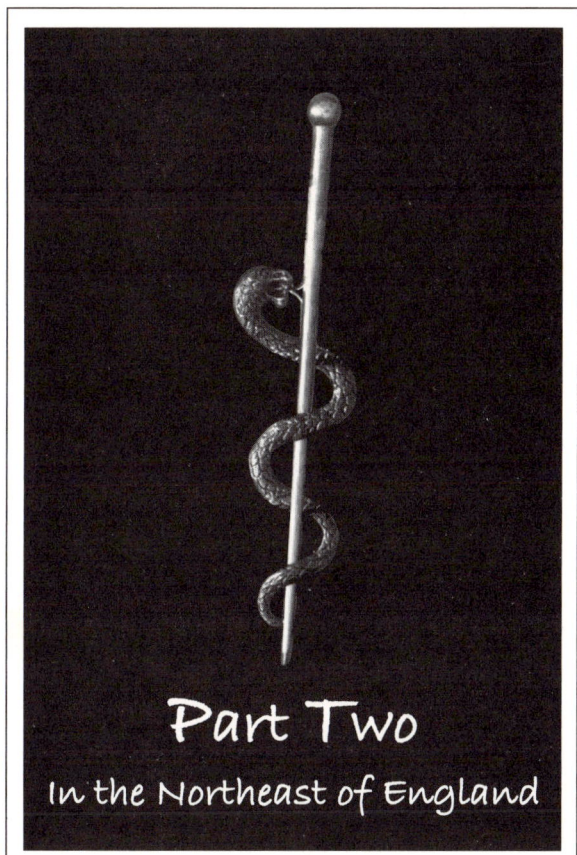

Part Two

In the Northeast of England

The short flight from Akaba to Cairo was hardly noticed
by Jones, as he contemplated recent events. A few hours
later, he boarded a British Airways 737 headed for home. The
brass serpent miniature was tucked securely into his still-dusty
satchel, which he carried with him onto the plane. A few minutes later, the aircraft took off and headed north.

Jones gazed down at the city disappearing behind the port
wing. His thoughts once again traversed the events of the last
few days. Receiving the miniature; meeting Nasir; Norman's
snakebite; they all had passed as if in an instant. Once again he
was leaving the region that meant so much to so many members of his family. Grandfather Alex had loved the area. Uncle
William and Cousin Colman had enjoyed Cairo immensely,
until they died there. In earlier years, Jones and his wife, Helen,
had also enjoyed meeting the various tribes of the region. They
had mastered one or two variations of the native tongue, which
made their work so much easier.

Now he was heading home, leaving behind all the happenings of recent days, but carrying with him a most treasured

possession. At least there would be no deadly snakes in cold, wet England. Jones relaxed, as the 737's flight path went along the east coast of Israel, swept over the edge of Turkey, on into Greece, and then home to England.

Helen, a tall, thin woman with a careworn but beautiful face, was there waiting for him as he walked down the gangway from the plane. The couple embraced for quite a long time, both relieved to find themselves in each other's arms once again.

At Gatwick, clearing customs was a mere formality. Soon they were driving to Milton Keynes in the family's Ford. Their conversation eventually came around to his expedition.

"There is something I want you to see," said Jones. "My recent find has made the trip very much worthwhile, but I don't want you to see it until we get home." Helen had to be restrained from reaching into the satchel, which never left Jones's side.

"We had a visitor from the home office in your absence," she said. "You are to ring them as soon as you get home."

"Anything in particular they wanted?" asked Jones.

"Not really. They just wanted to speak with you as soon as possible."

After the family reunion was over, the presents were given, the funny stories were told, and the two children were whisked off to bed, Jones was able to begin a detailed description of his Arabian adventure. Helen was enthralled by the story and especially its high point, the revealing of the original brass serpent. At which point, Jones brought forth the miniature.

"Take a look at this," he said. Helen looked the item over carefully, but she was not overly impressed. "Now bring it over here and look at the miniature again under this light."

Jones arranged both the overhead light and a table lamp to focus on the miniature. Helen looked and looked at the object. Suddenly, she appeared to be grasped by a force emanating from the serpent. It held her in its power for a few moments, and then Jones switched off the table lamp and the force holding his wife quickly abated.

"Why, it is just wonderful," said Helen. "If only our family had known about this. Then your father and your uncle and—"

"It's too late for them," Jones cut in. "What we have here may help save others, although we do not have any dangerous snakes in our country."

"You're right," said Helen. "So what use can it be here?"

"In God's time there will be a use for it," responded Jones. "This will have to be our little secret for now. No one must know about it, not even the children. We must protect the miniature at all times."

"The brass serpent was mentioned several times in the Bible—even Jesus referred to it," said Helen. "Let's look it up."

"Tell you what," said Jones, "look up the word Nehushtan."

"Ah! The word the Arabs used for the brass serpent," added Helen, reaching for the concordance. "Yes, here is the reference: second book of Kings, chapter eighteen, verse four. Find it for me," she said.

Jones found the reference and read it out to her. "Hezekiah removed the high places and broke the images. He cut down the groves and broke in pieces the brass serpent that Moses had made, for in those days the children of Israel did burn incense to it, and called it Nehushtan."

"If the people were still worshipping it all those centuries after Moses, then Nehushtan must have retained its ancient power to heal," said Helen. "Or perhaps there were other powers that it possessed which endangered the nation."

"Hezekiah must have seen the danger it posed and had it destroyed," said Jones. "Fortunately or unfortunately, another Nehushtan does exist."

"If only we had known about this a few years ago," said Helen.

"Well, we know quite a lot about it now," Jones responded.

"What's this?" exclaimed Helen. A newspaper cutting, wrinkled and worn, had dropped out of the leaves of the Bible. "Another one of your father's tidbits of information, no doubt." She casually opened the item and then paused, "You won't believe this!"

"What have you found now? Another article about the Ark of the Covenant, is it?"

"It begins with the title, 'Ancient Relic in Milan.' Then it says, some believe that Hezekiah did not destroy Nehushtan. At one of the most ancient churches in Italy, there allegedly exists the relic of Moses. According to the parishioners, Nehushtan sits today in the Basilica of Sant'Ambrogio. In AD 1000, Archbishop Arnolfo is said to have brought it to Milan, Italy. The object is located on top of a column on the left side of the central nave. It has reportedly been attributed with healing powers and a role in Judgment Day."

"How on earth could we have missed seeing that?" said Jones.

"Probably because we have been using the New English Bible, and this is the King James version," said Helen.

"Well, I take a view completely opposite to what the article says," said Jones in a heated fashion. "I have seen Nehushtan, or at least a copy of it, and Nehushtan is certainly not in Milan. Although one of these days I may visit Milan, just to satisfy my curiosity."

Their conversation turned to listing the deaths of their many relatives due to snakebite. Lastly, they remembered Helen's close call with death, when she suffered from snakebite in Beersheba. Deep in reflection, they finally retired to bed.

13

Early next morning, the bedside telephone rang. Helen answered the call. Reaching across the bed, she roused Jones, "It's for you."

Jones reluctantly took the phone from her. "Jones speaking."

"Jones? This is Colonel Basted at the home office. I want you to come up to London this afternoon. We have a problem that needs your background knowledge and experience."

"Yes, Colonel," responded Jones, now awake and aware of the immediacy of the situation. "I can be in London by three. Does that suit you?"

"Yes, that will do admirably," said Basted. "We will see you at three then."

Jones returned the telephone to Helen. "That was old Colonel Blasted at the home office."

"I thought that his name was Basted," said Helen.

"It is," confirmed Jones. "After working with him for a year, I discovered that the men had a more suitable name for him."

"I see," said Helen.

Jones arrived at the home office promptly at three. He was ushered into a large office with World War II pictures covering its walls. Basted was seated in a large, comfortable chair, and he gestured toward a chair of a more basic variety for Jones.

"Glad you could spare the time," Basted began cordially. Then his voice changed to a more serious tone. "We really do have a problem."

"Oh, yes?"

"This is highly confidential," said Basted. "You may have seen the newscasts about mysterious deaths in the mines of northeast England."

"Only briefly."

"Well, it turns out that these deaths are due to snakebite."

"Snakebite?" gasped Jones.

"How this has happened, we just don't know at present. We told the press that it may be a case of poisoning by noxious substances that had previously been stored in the mines. But believe me, the miners were all killed by snakebite."

"Most interesting," Jones pondered the new information.

"Snakes are your forte, are they not?" asked Basted. "People much higher up the ladder than I have put forward your name for the job. Will you take it on?"

"It sounds fascinating," said Jones. "I'm pleased that you asked me, and I would be glad to take on the job."

"It's a uniform job, I'm afraid." said Basted. "The mines have been sealed off by army units, but you will have a free hand once you are on site."

"My wife, Helen, has firsthand experience in this field. Could she assist me? She is ex-army and still has her uniform. Also, there is the matter of pay."

"Helen can certainly assist you. All expenses will be paid,

and you will receive a large bonus when you complete the investigation. We have but one request. You must keep this thing out of the press at all costs."

"Do we have a local contact?" asked Jones.

"Yes. Your contact is Major Philips, ex-RAMC. You may have met up with him during your time in the service."

"Yes, I do recall Major Philips," said Jones in a more subdued tone. How could he forget Philips? Major Philips was a man who took unnecessary risks. Jones thought to himself, "Perhaps he has changed. On the other hand, he could be a liability. Time will tell."

"So there it is then," said Basted. "Pick up your warrant and all the relevant details from my secretary on the way out. And," he paused, "good luck!"

Jones departed the office deep in thought. What had he got himself into? How could it be that he left Arabia with one problem on his mind, and now here he was engulfed in a very similar one? He remembered his dream vividly—the fight against the black knight and the dragon; the people pressing in on him for help. And now someone else needed his help. Snakes again! Where was it all leading? With his mind in turmoil, Jones headed home as evening descended across the London skyline.

"So, what was that all about?" asked Helen.

"There is a serious problem," said Jones. "Something we need to research together."

They went into the study. After checking that none of the children were around, he told Helen about the mysterious deaths and their cause. "This is very hush-hush," said Jones. "No one knows about it. To keep you on your toes, Basted has agreed to let you work with me on this case."

"That's wonderful!" exclaimed Helen. "It will be nice to work with you for a change, instead of hearing about your adventures when they are all over."

"That's what I thought. Go and dig out your old lieutenant's uniform. Oh, that reminds me. I will also need full uniform for this job. Can you get mine out of mothballs, too?"

Helen scurried away to unearth their respective uniforms.

"They look quite tidy, considering," said Jones as he inspected his old uniform.

"Considering mine hasn't been used for twelve years, it is quite tidy. So where exactly are we heading?" asked Helen, as she brushed the uniforms.

"To the northeast of England," said Jones. "A place called Chester-le-Street will be our center of operation."

"I used to work in Durham before I met you," said Helen. "I can interpret the dialect for you if you have any problems."

"Do you really want to come with me?" asked Jones. "I have a feeling there could be real danger for us both."

"You and your hunches," she said, remembering the many times her husband's premonitions had been right. "I'm ready, willing, and able!"

"I know that," responded Jones, "but we are talking about snakes, not sex."

"When do we leave?" she asked.

"Tomorrow morning, at the latest."

"Then we have a lot of preparations to make. I will tell the children that we are off on a working holiday. Meet you back here in an hour."

They parted to make their own preparations for the trip. When Helen returned to the study, Jones was flipping through various resource books. He packed all of the reference material he might need into a box and placed the covered miniature on an adjacent table.

At sunrise, the Joneses packed all of their essentials into their Ford and headed north on the Ml motorway. As they drove along, they discussed the various ways poisonous snakes could have been brought into the area. Had someone illegally imported a snake, or a pair of snakes? Had a snake come in on a fruit ship? Had a continental driver accidentally picked up a dangerous hitchhiker? How on earth could a snake find its way into a mine?

They discussed the likelihood that the miners were really killed by poisonous snakes, snakes that no one appeared to have seen. Could snakes actually thrive in mines? What would they drink, and what would they eat? Why were the snake-bites so lethal? Why was anti-venom serum not working? It appeared that there was very little information to go on, except that the miners died of snakebite. This investigation could be a deadly mission.

14

As they drove up the A1 north of Ferrybridge, Helen remembered her time in County Durham. "I recall that Chester-le-Street has a famous inn called the Lambton Worm. It would be quite nostalgic for me to visit it."

"Would you like to stay there?" inquired Jones.

"Yes, please."

"Then, just point me in the right direction when we get there."

As they approached Chester-le-Street, Helen began giving directions. "Just take this next exit on the left. Second turn on your left. Right at this roundabout. One hundred yards on your left. Slow down. Here it is."

"Quite straight forward, really," quipped Jones, as he turned into the small parking space. "It looks like a nice hotel. What are those funny pictures?" asked Jones, referring to a billboard near the entrance.

"Cartoons of the Lambton Worm, I suspect," said Helen. "The place appears to have had quite a facelift since my last visit." Helen got out of the car and went into the hotel seeking accommodations. A few minutes later, she emerged with the manager. Jones was stretching his legs beside their vehicle.

"Mr. Jackie Bolam, meet my husband, Major William Jones," said Helen.

"Glad to meet you," said Jones. "I see that you have already met my wife."

"A reet bonny lass, and no mistake," responded Jackie.

The two men took an instant liking to each other, even though Jones was not sure whether or not Jackie had been complementary to his wife. They removed the luggage and boxes from the car and were assisted by Jackie to a most spacious and comfortable room.

"Ye can spread oot here as much as you like. Divent worry if ye make a mess," said Jackie. "Dinner is at six, but we can fix you summat up when ye like."

Helen and Jones quickly unpacked their belongings. The room was more than adequate for their needs. Feeling hungry, both for food and for information, the couple went downstairs to quiz Jackie. Their conversation soon turned to the mysterious deaths in the mines.

"There's been nuthin like it in livin' memory," said Jackie.

"What do you think is going on?" asked Helen.

"I've nee idea, missus," said Jackie, "but it's mighty peculiar. There's been nuthin like it since the Lambton Worm."

"That's the name of this hotel," said Jones.

"That's reet," said Jackie. "It used to be called the Chester Rest House, but we figured oot that we wad get more tourists by changing the name."

They explored various avenues of local history with Jackie but didn't come up with anything that would give them a clue as to what was going on in the local mines. Finally, the couple retired to their room to set up a working area complete with maps, reference books, notes, and lists of questions that needed to be asked. When all was prepared, they decided that they were, after all, really hungry. They went back downstairs to the restaurant, where their host was just finishing his meal.

"So, you'll be here for a while?" probed Jackie.

"Yes, we are doing some research up at the old Birtley Mine tomorrow," Jones responded. "After that, we may be exploring other locations in this area."

"Mining experts, are we?"

"Not really," said Helen. "We have to check various security items stored in the mines—chemicals and the like. We will need an early start in the morning, so a call at six thirty would be appreciated."

"Nee problem," said Jackie, handing Helen a menu. "Now, what can I do you for?"

They took their time selecting from the excellent menu and savored every bite of their meal.

Jackie returned to top up their coffees. "Everything allreet?"

"That was some meal," responded Jones.

"Most enjoyable," added Helen. "I think a bit of fresh air and an early night would just about do it for me."

"So we'll say good night to you, Jackie," said Jones, as they prepared to leave.

"Good neet," Jackie nodded his head.

Eventually the couple found their way back to their room after a casual walk in the rather cool evening air. Weariness began to creep over them, and they settled into bed.

"It's been a long day," said Helen.

"Should be a most interesting day tomorrow," Jones yawned, as he switched off the bedside lamp. "Good neet."

15

They were just beginning to stir when the six thirty call sounded. Jones was first to respond and headed immediately into the shower. Helen followed two minutes later, easing herself into the shower alongside her husband. They held each other in a lingering embrace, as the warm water splashed over their naked bodies. Jones was already beginning to focus on the challenge of the work ahead, so he absently broke free of Helen's loving embrace.

"Catch you later," he said, as he moved on to his shaving routine.

They had just finished dressing in their uniforms when a simple breakfast arrived.

"I'll have toast to start with," said Helen.

"Suits me fine," said Jones. "I'll have everything that you can't manage."

After breakfast, they sat for a few minutes sipping coffee and gathering their thoughts for the day. Eventually Jones made a move to leave, and Helen tidied up the breakfast tray and placed it outside the door. They looked at each other, exchanged a brief kiss, and said in unison, "Let's go!"

They were leaving the hotel when Jackie spotted them. "Well I nivver. Smart enough to gan to a funeral."

"No funeral for us today, but we do expect to be rather busy. We should be back sometime this evening," said Helen. "Please leave our room untouched. There are important and confidential documents there, and we would prefer they were not moved."

"Nee problem missus," said Jackie. "I'll see you the neet."

They got into their car and turned north out of the parking lot. Within two miles, they found themselves at the old Birtley Mine. A squad of soldiers formed a barrier at the colliery gate. Jones adjusted his officer's cap and emerged from the vehicle. The corporal of the guard saluted him, and he returned salute. "Major Jones?"

Jones nodded.

"Major Philips is expecting you, Sir," said the corporal. "You can park at the office over there." He indicated a small site office.

Jones returned to Helen in the car and drove slowly over to the parking area. As they emerged from the vehicle, a bright and cheerful greeting met their ears.

"Jones—and Helen, too! How nice to see you both," Philips beamed. He shook Jones' hand warmly and then gave Helen a very gentle kiss. "Well, how are you both? How many children do you have now? Two? Or is it three?"

"Just the two for now," responded Jones. Jones was taken aback by Philip's warmth, but he responded in a good spirit. "I never expected to see you again," he said cheerily. "Well, not in uniform, not after your last escapade."

"Well, that is a part of my distant past," Philips admitted. "The army decided to give me one more chance, especially since I have some knowledge of mines. So here I am again, still at it, so to speak."

"And here we are, too," Helen chimed in.

They moved inside the site office, where Philips pointed to a map pinned to a bare wall. "This is what we have so far. During the last year, there have been safety inspections carried out in all the local mines by mining deputies. Unfortunately, seven of them have died." He pointed to various spots on the map to indicate the mines concerned. "Three here at Birtley. Two at Shiney Row, there. And two at a very old mine called Old Smokey, over there toward Penshaw."

"Deaths at all three places?" asked Jones.

"Actually, that is what we originally thought," said Philips. "Lately, we have been researching the movements of these people before they died, and we found that, although the deputies visited each site, it was always Old Smokey that they toured last."

"So the problem is at Old Smokey," responded Helen. "Why do you have soldiers here at Birtley?"

"We made this a safety issue in the press," said Philips. "The army's presence assures them that we are taking the deaths seriously."

"Well, I would like to see each mine for myself," said Jones.

"Certainly, old boy. I will give you a royal tour. Put on these safety hats, and we'll start right here at Birtley."

The trio, lead by Philips, made their way to the first mine-shaft, where they were met by Jim, the under manager.

"A quick tour of the facility, if you please, Jim," said Philips.

"These people are from the home office, checking up on mine safety and security. They must be shown everything. Answer all questions. Hold nothing back! Got it?"

"I'll do my best, sir," said Jim.

They followed Jim at a respectable distance, stopping occasionally to ask him various questions to authenticate their cover. What was done here? What is stored in those containers? Why is that door sealed up? They kept up the pretense throughout the tour of the mine. Then, they came to the main point of their inquiry.

"It was so sad to learn of the recent deaths here," Helen began. "Were those men friends of yours?"

"Aye, missus. Fred Kimberley was a guid friend of mine. We were marras!" said Jim.

"Were you there when he first became ill?" asked Helen

"Aye, missus. We had just left here and checked into Old Smokey, where we normally have our bate. He seemed all reet at the time, and then, all of a sudden, he went all queer like," said Jim. "So we decided right then to call the ambulance."

"Had you been anywhere near the dangerous goods store here at Birtley before you went to the other mine?" asked Jones.

"Aye, come to think of it, we had done a reet good job there."

"Did he touch anything while he was in the store?" asked Helen.

"Not without his gloves on, he didn't," Jim responded.

"What about the other two who died? Did you know either of them?" Philips asked.

"No, sir," said Jim.

"Do you know what they were doing before they were taken ill?" Helen inquired.

"No, missus. They were on a different security shift than me," said Jim. "A didn't even kna tha names."

"Well, if you do remember any details that might help our investigation, you know where you can find me," said Philips. "Anything at all." The trio left Jim to his duties.

"Like I said," said Philips, "the problem appears to be at Old Smokey and not here. But before we go to Shiney Row, we can have a cup of coffee. Then we'll head down the way by one o'clock."

As they approached the Shiney Row mine, they were confronted by another squad of soldiers guarding the entrance. Philip's military Land Rover was recognized immediately by the soldier at the gate and waved through. Jones and Helen followed closely behind in their vehicle. At the pit head they were met by the ex-manager, Billy Longstaff.

"Now then Billy, how are we today?" began Philips.

"Am reet canny," said Billy, indicating that he was very well.

"We have important officials from the home office visiting today," Philips continued. "They need to know everything about this mine—its safety record and all that you know about the deaths that occurred here."

"Well, for a start, the deaths never bloody occurred here," said Billy angrily.

"What exactly happened, then?" asked Helen in a concerned tone.

The female voice calmed Billy down. "We did wor usual check of the dangerous goods store. Then we had a good look arooned, checking to see if we'd had any breck-ins," continued Billy. "I said to wor Neil, let's have wuh bate here, before we gan doon tuh Auld Smokey. But ye kna him, he wadn't listen. Desperate to get doon tuh Auld Smokey, he was."

"Why was that?" asked Helen.

"Well, him and yon Jimmy Waddle had this thing aboot pontoon. They always played at bate time, when they could. Anyway, they left here, and that's the last time I saw wor Neil alive."

"Was Neil well before he left here?" asked Helen sympathetically.

"Why aye, missus. He was as reet as rain."

"And he never touched anything in your dangerous goods store?" Philips asked.

"Not withoot his bloody gloves on, he didn't," responded Billy.

"I think that we had better start with a look at this dangerous goods store of yours," said Philips. "Then, you can show us around the rest of the mine."

The group went through the formality of inspecting the mine. The tour seemed endless, but it had to be done to give the impression of leaving no stone unturned, as it were. All the while, in their hearts they knew that the danger lay at the Old Smokey mine. By late afternoon they had completed the inspection. They took their leave of Billy, who was still grieving over the loss of "wor Neil."

"No point in heading down to Old Smokey now," said Philips. "We can tackle that situation first thing in the morning."

The Joneses left Philips to his own devices and took their time driving the few miles back to the hotel.

"They all appear to be very safety conscious," Helen began.

"Yes, I noticed that," said Jones. "They always wore their

safety gloves when handling and checking the dangerous goods."

"Whatever happened, whatever killed those poor men must be at this Old Smokey Mine," Helen deduced.

"Did you notice that both Jim and Billy mentioned that the men were going to have their bate," said Jones. "What exactly is a bate?"

"You might call it their lunch, dear," responded Helen.

"Well, whatever they call it, they chose a bad place for it," responded Jones. "We can look over the situation there very carefully tomorrow."

"I can't wait to get out of this uniform and get into a hot bath," Helen sighed.

"I might join you for that," said Jones, as they drove into the hotel parking lot.

16

It was around nine the next morning that the Joneses, following Philip's vehicle, found their way to the Old Smokey Mine. After the customary halt, check, and salute, they entered a small complex of derelict buildings. They were nicely matched by a view of the nearby Penshaw Monument in its incomplete state.

The caretaker, Norman Fairfield, a much older man than the previous gentlemen, greeted them. "What have you brought along today, Major Philips?"

"These are experts from the home office," responded Philips. "Meet Major Jones and his wife, Helen. They need to know everything about this mine from A to Z."

"For starters," said Jones, "why exactly is the mine called Old Smokey?"

"Well, it's like this. In the olden days there was a good mine here. The first level of coal was brilliant—even exported it to southern parts, so they say. When that seam was worked out, they decided to sink a shaft a bit lower. They found coal all reet, but there was one accident after another. A lot of fires were mysteriously ignited. Thank God, no one was killed."

"And what was the cause of the fires?"

"Neebody knows," said Norman in very clear English. "Personally, I think it was, and still is, a poor seam of coal. What made it worse was the dampness in the second seam. Even now there is running water in there."

"When did the mine cease producing coal?" asked Helen.

"Well before my time, I can tell you," said Norman. "I retired from work in 1960, and took on this job part-time. I've been here ever since."

"You must be getting on a bit, Norman," said Philips. "Why do the owners keep you on?"

"Why man, I'm the only one who knows where everything is!" Norman joked.

"Well, Norman, these people want to know exactly what you have here," said Philips. "I want you to show us everything, every nook and cranny."

The trio once again experienced a grand tour of the mine, but this time their eyes drank in every little detail. The dangerous substance store was opened and inspected carefully. Detailed lists were scrutinized and omissions noted. No room went unchecked. Every corridor was followed to its end. They descended by lift, and the first seam was also thoroughly checked.

"Where did the security men have their lunch?" asked Helen.

"They usually had their bate in that little office over there," said Norman. He opened the door for his guests to enter. The room was bare, except for a few basic chairs and one simple table. "Nothing to see really. Even less to see at the second seam."

The four of them entered the lift to take them down to the next level. As they entered the seam, Jones noticed a faint smell of smoke.

"I can smell smoke," said Helen.

Jones nodded his agreement.

"Welcome to Auld Smokey," said Norman.

They walked slowly past broken pieces of machinery and then entered and searched each office that they came across. All was quiet. The smell of smoke had disappeared.

"No sign of any smoke here," said Philips, looking to Norman for an explanation.

"Nothing but the occasional whiff of it over these last twelve years," said Norman.

"What's that room over there?" asked Helen.

"Nothing but an old bate room," said Norman. "When a big inspection is on, the lads usually sit in there."

The door was wide open, so they entered and stood quietly in the centre of the room. Soon they became aware of a rustling sound.

"What's that?" queried Helen in an alarmed tone.

"Nowt but a rat," said Norman.

"There's a funny smell, too," Helen was still concerned.

"So there is," agreed Norman.

"Faintly smoky, don't you think?" asked Philips.

"I hardly notice it these days," Norman responded.

"It is! It is a distinctly smoky smell," affirmed Helen.

"It hasn't been noticeable anywhere else except in here," Jones commented.

"I've never noticed that before," said Norman. "Anyway, there's nowt else down here."

"We could do with a detailed map of each of the mine

seams," said Jones. "We need to know the function of each section."

"Some of the older maps of the area would come in handy, too," said Philips.

"I'll give you all I've got," said Norman, "when we get back up top."

As they made their way back to the lift, they brought up the matter of the deaths.

"Were you on duty when the men were taken ill?" Helen asked.

"Aye, missus," said Norman, slipping back to his normal mode of speech. "It was a strange affair. They arrived on site and had their bate; each time, and, as they prepared to carry on with their work, one of them would be taken queer."

"Just one of them?" queried Jones.

"Aye, it was truly amazing. Only one each time."

"Can you account for that?"

"I can't, but it was always in the bate rooms that something happened," said Norman. "They got poisoned somehow."

The trio looked at each other. Clearly Norman was not aware of the source of the poison.

"And what is worse, none of them lived to tell the tale," added Jones.

"That's reet," said Norman. "Now I just stand guard over the place and watch carefully over the different inspectors who come to the mine. One thing that I won't let them do is have their bate here."

"I think that's very wise in the present situation," said Philips. "We will take a good look at these plans of yours Norman. Expect us here tomorrow, bright and early."

They emerged from the lift and helped themselves to all

of Norman's site plans. Then, they headed to Philip's Birtley headquarters in their respective vehicles.

"Lots to think about tonight over this situation," said Philips. "I will keep the maps tonight, and you can have them tomorrow. OK?"

"Yes, a good night's rest will do Helen and me a lot of good," said Jones.

"We can make a fresh start tomorrow."

"It's been a long and smoky day," said Helen. "I haven't got a scent that can compete with the smell of smoke."

"I'm really famished," said Jones. "I could eat a horse."

"Not in the bate room, you couldn't," quipped Philips.

"Not without your gloves on, either," said Helen.

"We'll meet at Old Smokey in the morning," said Philips. "Say around nine? You can find your own way there."

The Joneses walked to their car, and Philips waved them a cheery goodbye as they drove away.

"We've got a lot to think about," said Jones.

"But we will be able to see the situation a lot more clearly when we get a hold of those maps," said Helen.

17

They arrived back at the Lambton Worm at around six in the evening. Wanting to avoid any conversation with Jackie, they hurried quickly toward their room. They were unlucky, however, as Jackie had been waiting for them just inside the vestibule.

"Had a long day have we?" he began.

"Long and difficult," said Jones trying to brush past him.

"Aye, ah can tell that from the look on yuh faces."

"We do feel rather tired," said Helen, as Jones continued on toward their room. "Major Jones is also quite hungry."

"Give me an hour, and I'll have the chef prepare something reet tasty for you."

"That would be very nice," said Helen in a clipped tone. "Say around seven then?"

"Aboot siven," Jackie confirmed.

Helen nodded and then continued on to the room, avoiding any further conversation. She entered the room to find Jones running the bath taps. Clearly, he intended to have a bath, which was most unusual for him.

"I need a real soak," he said.

"After me then?" suggested Helen, carefully removing her uniform and then throwing off her remaining clothes, wanting to be first into the bath.

"I'll give you five minutes to yourself, and then I'm coming in."

"There is not really enough room for the two of us," said Helen as she dipped her toe in the hot water.

"We'll manage somehow," Jones teased, hinting at ulterior motives.

"We are not in Cairo now," Helen grinned, referring to a previous lovemaking experience.

"Five minutes, and I'm coming in," repeated Jones.

Helen sank into the warm waters, while Jones slowly removed his uniform. He hung it up and gave it a gentle brushing. He found Helen's uniform and treated it with even more respect than his own. As he brushed, he became aware of a faint aroma. He murmured to himself, "Old Smokey." Then, remembering his wife in the bath, he called out, "Ready or not, here I come."

There was just enough room in the bath for the two of them, one at each end. However, they eventually found another more suitable arrangement for making love.

Over and hour later, the Joneses emerged from their room wearing casual attire. The couple sauntered into the restaurant at seven thirty. They were met at the door by an agitated Jackie.

"I thought that you weren't coming here for a minute," he fumed.

"I found something quite interesting to study," said Jones. "I hope that you haven't been waiting too long."

"He can work quite quickly when he has to," added Helen.

"Now, where is this feast?" said Jones. "I'm starving."

Jackie had indeed prepared for them a sumptuous meal of chicken and pork with all of the trimmings. The pair took considerable time over the dinner, giving it the justice it deserved. All the while Jackie hovered about, catering to their every whim. Eventually, his desire to converse with the Joneses overcame him. He took the liberty of sitting down with the couple when he delivered the last round of coffee.

"I believe I may be able to help you," he began in clear English. "You've been at the mines again today?"

"How did you guess?" asked Helen.

"Well, apart from the smell on your uniforms, a few of the locals have noticed the military lady gannin aboot the place."

"Have you anything new to tell us?" Helen asked.

"Nothing new, but my old man used to work in the Birtley Mine. He also did a couple of years on security at Auld Smokey," Jackie continued. "He told us lads many a tale aboot the pits in the auld days."

"It is very kind of you to offer," said Helen, "but tonight we just want to relax and take in the atmosphere of your hotel."

"The Lambton Worm," Jones began. "Why is The Lambton Worm the name for this hotel?"

"Well, it certainly attracts the tourists for one thing," said Jackie. "And it's a much better name than the auld name, The Chester Rest House."

"This Lambton Worm, what do you know about it?" asked Jones.

"Well, the story of the Lambton Worm used to be printed on the back of our menus," said Jackie. "Since the refurbishment, it has been dropped. Tell you what! I'll see if I can find an auld copy."

Jackie disappeared into his office and soon reappeared with a menu in his hand. "Here it is. It says here that there was an auld song entitled "The Lambton Worm." It was first sung in a pantomime in 1867."

"That is most kind of you, Jackie," said Helen as she looked over the song written on the back of the old menu.

THE LAMBTON WORM

One Sunday mornin' Lambton went
A-fishin' in the Wear;
An' catched a fish upon he's heuk,
He thowt leuk't varry queer.
But whatt'n a kind ov fish it was
Young Lambton cudden't tell.
He waddn't fash te carry'd hyem,
So he hoyed it in a well.

Whisht! lads, haad yor gobs,
An' aa'll tell ye' aall an aaful story,
Whisht! lads, haad yor gobs,
An aa'll tell ye 'boot the worm.

Noo Lambton felt inclined te gan an' fight i'
    foreign wars.
He joined a troop ov knights that cared
For neither woonds nor scars,
An' off he went te Palestine,
Where queer things him befel,
An varry seun forgat aboot
The queer woorm i' the well.

But the woorm got fat an' growed an' growed,
An' growed an aaful size;
He'd greet big teeth, a greet big gob,
An' greet big goggley eyes.
An' when at neets he craaled aboot
Te pick up bits o' news,
If he felt dry upon the road,
He milked a dozen coos.

This feorful woorm would often feed
On caalves an' lambs an' sheep,
An' swally little bairns alive
When they laid doon te sleep.
An' when he'd eaten aall he cud
An' he had had he's fill,
Re craaled away an' lapped he's tail
Ten times roond Pensher Hill.

The news of this myest aaful woorm
An' his queer gannins on
Seun crossed the seas, gat t'e the ears
Ov brave an' bowld Sor John.
So hyem he cam an' catched the beast
An' cut 'im in twe haalves,
An' that seun stopped he's eatin' bairns
An' sheep an' lambs an' caalves.

So noo ye knaa hoo aall the foalks
On byeth sides ov the wear
Lost lots o' sheep an' lots o' sleep

An' leeved i' mortal feor.
So let's hey one te brave Sor John
That kept the bairns frae harm,
Saved coos an' caalves by myekin' haalves
O' the famis Lambton Woorm.

Noo, lads, aa'll haad me gob.
That's aall Aa knaâ aboot the story
Ov Sor John's clivvor job wi' the aaful
Lambton Woorm.

—*The Lambton Worm* was written by
C. M. Leumane and first sung in a
pantomime at the Old Tyne Theatre in 1867.

"I don't think that my husband will make much sense of this," said Helen.

"There's nowt to it!" said Jackie. "John Lambton, as a lad, caught a queer fish. It might have been a sort of worm. He throws it doon a well. Later on, this worm grows very big, big enough to catch and kill large animals. John, now Sir John, is away in Palestine on a crusade. He hears aboot the worm. He comes home and kills it."

"Well, I understood that all right," said Jones.

"Aroond these parts most people say that there is more to the song than just a legend," Jackie added. "One thing is certain sure, and that is the Lambton family have some sort of family curse on them. There have been some queer deaths among that family, too, just like this carryon at the mines."

"What have you heard about the deaths at the mines?" asked Jones, suddenly very interested in the conversation.

"Well, the locals say that they have been hiding dangerous gas cylinders at Auld Smokey," said Jackie. "Maybe from the first World War. So that could be the real cause of the miners' deaths. It could be the chemicals that they keep at the mine. Well it could be!"

"Very interesting," said Jones. "We do need to know of any rumors going around. Please keep us informed."

"Certainly," said Jackie. "Is there anything else I can help you with?"

"Not tonight, Jackie. Thanks!" said Helen. "We have a later start tomorrow, so we would like breakfast in our room in the morning, say at eight?"

They rose from their table, bid Jackie goodnight, and went to their room. Jones hastened into the bathroom, preparing himself for bed. Helen tidied up the room and then sat down by the reading light to look at the song again. After a few minutes, she tired of the task and prepared herself for bed. Upon her return from the bathroom, she found her husband fast asleep.

Helen slipped quietly into bed alongside her husband. Jones was deep in sleep, so she flicked off the bedside light and settled into the soft sheets. But sleep would not come. The day's activities filled her mind. The words of the song created all sorts of strange images in her head. What could be gleaned from it all? She felt overwhelmed and finally fell into a fitful asleep.

18

Helen dreamed of many things: the dark mines, the ominous rustling, and Penshaw Hill with its monument adorned by a huge yellow ribbon. Snatches of the Lambton Worm song came and went. She was winding the handle of a well, but she couldn't reach the end of the rope to see what was there. Then, she was fishing and catching nothing but miners' safety helmets. A snake was reaching out to bite her, and she was cowering away from it. There was a miner offering her a sandwich, but his hands were black with coal dust. She was looking down into a well and saw no reflection of the sky in the deep water. Suddenly the well began to grow bigger and bigger, and she was falling into it. Something touched her, and she jumped into wakefulness. It was her husband calling her.

"Helen! Helen, the alarm has gone off," said Jones. "Time to get up."

"What an awful night I've had."

"What about me?" responded Jones. "You kicked me around the bed like a football. Are you all right?"

"Give me an extra ten minutes, and I'll be OK," said Helen.

"Get your shower and shave, and then I'll come." Helen relaxed and stretched between the sheets. What a horrible night it had been. Nothing had been resolved. She was more muddled in her thinking than ever. She rested, browsing slowly through the pieces of remembered dreams. She began to feel apprehension about going into the mines, a kind of apprehension that she had never experienced before. Then, there was that well. She could see it again in her mind. It grew and grew to an awful size. What did the well have to do with the mines?

"Bathroom's clear," said Jones as he entered the room from the bathroom.

Helen arose and pensively drifted into the bathroom. The sharpness of a cool shower soon brought her to her senses. Breakfast arrived. She gulped down two cups of coffee, which helped her pull herself together. Feeling more composed, she finished dressing, slowly putting on her uniform. Then she caught her breath, as a whiff of Old Smokey reached her nostrils. It was quarter to nine, and Jones was standing at the door waiting.

The drive to Old Smokey went by in silence. As they slowly approached the mine gates, her apprehensive husband said, "Are you all right now?"

"Sorry, my dear husband," said Helen. "Have I been neglecting you?"

"No! Not really. I like time to think, time to think things through, just as you do," said Jones. "It is just that we need to be on our toes today. We must get to grips with this problem. We are not here on a paid holiday, you know."

Philips was there waiting for them. He guided them into the small office. "I have been looking carefully over the maps," he said, "and I've found something interesting. We know that Norman showed us everything that he could in the mine.

However, I've found something on an old map that we didn't notice when we were down there." He pointed to a small offshoot in the second seam. "It appears that this spur was sealed off after some initial exploration was carried out."

"Let's ask Norman," said Helen, forcing herself to take more of an active interest.

Norman was hovering near the office, just in case he was needed. He expected to be consulted on anything involving "his" mine. They showed him the map and pointed out the offshoot. "That must have been sealed off well before my time," he said. "I've never noticed it."

"We had better take a closer look, then," said Philips.

As they donned their safety helmets, Helen said, "If you don't mind, I won't go down with you this time. I would like to take a little more time to study these maps."

"You just take it easy today," said Jones. "We won't be long." As they left the office, Jones said to the others, "She's had a rough night." The other two looked at each other, smiled knowingly, but made no comment. The three men descended in the lift to the second seam.

"I can smell the smoke quite clearly today," said Philips.

"Funny that," said Norman. "It's nivver been this bad for many a month."

They walked about one hundred meters into the second level.

"Here it is!" said Philips, pointing to a walled-off section.

"I remember it now," said Norman.

"Not exactly in good condition," commented Jones, as he felt a piece of wall cement crumble in his hands.

"Aye, it's a rough job, alreet," said Norman.

"I wonder why they sealed off this section," said Jones.

"Didn't do much of a job," said Norman.

"It may have been too damp for the miners to work in safety," said Philips. "We have to remember that miners didn't have the machinery available to them in those days that they have today."

"I think we should go further into this seam, just to see what the situation is at the coal face," said Jones.

"Follow me," said Norman. "When it gets too dangerous, we will have to stop."

The trio moved slowly forward, with Norman leading the way and pointing out pieces of interesting machinery as he went. Before long, they all noticed how damp it had become, but Norman pressed on. He eventually came to a dead stop when they encountered running water cutting across their path.

"Like I said, it can get a bit damp in here," Norman said. "We had better turn back before we have to swim." The three men turned around and quietly felt their way out until they came, once again, to the sealed-off section. The smell of smoke had increased.

"Look at that wall!" exclaimed Norman. "There's plenty of smoke coming out of that gap at the top."

The trio looked at each other with uncertainly. Jones pointed to the place where he had removed some cement. Smoke was seeping out of there, too. "I've got a bad feeling about this," he said.

"It's nowt to worry aboot," said Norman. "We get flare ups now and then. Mind you, it looks as though there is something going on behind that wall. We had better get out of here. Just follow me quickly, and mind how you go."

They swiftly covered the distance back to the lift shaft. As they stood in the rising cage, a distinct smell of smoke went with them. They emerged into the welcoming sunlight, but when they turned around to look back, wisps of black smoke could be seen rising into the air.

"It will settle in an hour or so," said Norman.

"Well, at least now I know why it is called Old Smokey," said Jones.

They walked together to the site office, where Helen was still poring over the old maps. "You're back early," she said.

"It got a bit smoky down there," quipped Philips. "So we've come up for a breath of fresh, northeast air."

"I have been looking at this area on the map," said Helen pointing to a region of the map. "The area just beyond here is called Caldwell."

"That's reet, missus," said Norman, forgetting Helen's rank. "There was a farm over there at one time, but it has been built over with retired miners homes."

"Do you know whether there was a well there at one time?" asked Helen.

"I've nee idea aboot that," said Norman. "It's not far to walk from here."

"It's a fine day, William. Let's go for a walk," suggested Helen.

"No! We can't just take time off like that," said Jones. "Anyway, we are both in uniform. We can drive around to the Caldwell area, if you like. But why? Why this sudden interest in wells?"

"While you were away, I studied those maps. I've seen something that I think that we should investigate," said Helen, showing persistence that Jones knew not to question.

"I have some writing to do," said Philips. "You two go on by yourselves. I'll be here when you get back."

19

Using the map, Helen navigated Jones to a specific region. They turned down a side road and found a set of six terraced houses. Jones drew his vehicle up to the last house on the street.

"Time to ask a few questions," said Helen. "You can come and give me moral support."

The house at the end of the terrace appeared to be rather rundown. Ramshackle allotments took over where the terrace ended. Jones knocked firmly on the front door. Chains rattled, bolts were drawn back, and the door swung open. A smart looking, square-shouldered pensioner greeted them. "What the heck do you want?"

Helen, taken aback, responded quietly, "We were wondering whether you knew anything about a well in this area."

"There's nee well in my garden," was the curt response.

"What about in those allotments over there?" asked Helen.

"Don't know. Never been in there for bloody years."

"Have you heard of the Caldwell area?" Helen persisted.

"Why aye, missus. You're in it. Look, why not gan over to them allotments ower there and have a look for yourself. There's nivver anybody aboot."

"Yes, we will do that," said Helen. "Thank you for your help."

"Fine, just leave me in peace," was the pensioner's final comment, as he slammed his door shut, followed by the slamming of a bolt into position and the rattling of a security chain.

"Not exactly a friendly type," said Jones.

"Nobody's perfect," responded Helen, remembering some of her husband's rougher moments.

They located the gate to the allotments and, upon entering, found themselves on an overgrown path with no end in sight. They wandered aimlessly down little cul-de-sacs, searching for someone to help them.

"Are you lost?" called a voice from a greenhouse.

"Yes, we are sort of lost," Helen responded. "Where are you?"

"Here!" said a very tall, bald-headed man, stepping out from his small greenhouse.

"We are looking for a well," said Helen.

"Well, well! You've come to the right place."

"You know where it is?" asked Helen.

"Yes, I do. As it happens, there's an old well at the bottom of this slope here. Would you like to see it?"

"That would be most helpful," said Helen.

"Are you both in the home guard?"

"No. We are actually here on Army business," said Jones.

"Didn't know the Army was interested in wells."

"Well, we are," said Helen, beginning to sense the intended humor.

"Walk this way," said the man, who seemed to be always on the verge of cracking a joke but never quite getting to the punch line.

The trio stepped through a gap in the allotment hedge and then followed a track down to the bottom of the slope. There immediately before them was a well, but it was in very poor condition, with many loose stones and crumbling cement. Jones was reminded instantly of the burial mound that he and Nasir found in Arabia.

"Here it is. Needs doing up, I'm afraid. This is a long way to come for a drink of water. If you'd mentioned it, I could have given you a bottle of pop from my greenhouse."

"Would this be the Caldwell that is referred to on my map?" Helen asked. "We would really like to know."

"I don't really know, missus, but it is the only well in this area. I should know, because I've lived in these parts all of my life."

"I would like to be able to see down into the well," said Helen, turning to her husband.

"Let's see if we can lift off the covering," said Jones to the man. Together, the two men wrestled with the covering, until finally they were able to edge it slowly to one side.

"Now, I must see into it," said Helen. She eased herself up onto the well's perimeter.

"It's a lang way doon if you are considering diving in."

"No, I just want to see to the bottom," said Helen. She positioned herself carefully and looked anxiously down into the well.

"What on earth are you looking for?" Jones asked with growing annoyance.

"There is no reflection of the sky," she said.

"That reet, missus," said the man. "There has nivver been

any water in that well, since the Lambton Worm was first hoyed doon it."

"You mean to tell me this is where the Lambton Worm came from?"

"Aye, that's possibly reet. All I know is that there has been nee water in that well since just after the time of Sir John Lambton."

"Do you really believe that there was a Lambton Worm?" said Jones sarcastically. "That's what I tell the kids hanging aroond the allotments. They believe anything like that these days. Main thing is it keeps them away from my greenhouse at neet."

"I wonder why there is no water in the well," said Helen.

"It's my opinion that the miners cut through the source of the water many decades ago, and so the well dried up."

"You mean the miners at the Old Smokey Mine?" asked Jones.

"Exactly."

"So according to you, the Lambton Worm's descendants could still be floating around in Old Smokey right now?" asked Helen.

"That's what I keep telling the kids."

"Well, I must say you have been very helpful," said Helen.

"Let's get the cover back in position before somebody falls in," said Jones.

"Or before the Lambton Worm gets oot," quipped the man.

The two of them secured the well cover, and the Joneses took their leave of its guardian.

"What a pleasant chap," said Helen.

"You're reet there missus," quipped Jones.

20

They drove back to Old Smokey and found Philips still engrossed in his paperwork. "Find anything?" he asked.

"Just an old well," said Jones, unwilling to share their queer findings. Was there any truth in what they had heard? Had they really found John Lambton's well?

"As I see it," said Philips, "we have two questions that we need to answer. First, what exactly killed those men? If it was snakebite, where are the snakes? Secondly, why does this mine smoke?"

"Home office research says that the men died of snakebite, a most venomous variety at that," said Jones. "We need to locate the snakes and destroy them."

"That may not be easy," said Philips. "This is quite a big mine."

"And there is no smoke without fire, as the saying goes. So we need to find out what is on fire in the mine," said Jones. "What's smoking in Old Smokey?"

"Perhaps the two things are related," Helen added her opinion.

"Could be," said Philips. "But let us tackle the fire issue first. We need to break through that wall on the second level and locate the fire, if there is one."

"I think you are right there," said Jones. "You can let the home office know what we intend to do. We'll see what they suggest. In the meantime, Helen and I can do a bit more investigating with regard to the deaths."

Helen and Jones left Philips to contact the home office while they looked around the site for Norman. They found him doing his rounds, methodically checking each building.

"Do you have a record of what everyone does daily on this site?" asked Jones.

"Aye!" said Norman. "It's my job to know who does what aroond here."

"Can you look up your records for the days those security men were taken ill?" Helen asked.

"Come over to the office, and I'll dig out the records," said Norman. He took them to a small office containing filing cabinets and little else. He took out three red files. "These are the ones you want. It's all in here."

"Well, I would like to know exactly where these men became ill," said Helen.

"That's easy," said Norman. "See here! All seven took their bate here, on this site. They used either the first or second level bate rooms, since there are water and power points in them. The men mainly used the first level room, because it still has decent furniture in it. Also, it is quite dry in there."

"We would like to see that room again, if you don't mind," said Helen.

"Nee problem, missus," said Norman, relapsing into his dialect.

They stopped in to see Philips on their way. "We are going back into the first level of the mine, just to take another look," said Jones. "Do you want to come with us?"

"Yes, but I need to go down to the second level, just to check the condition of that wall," said Philips. "The home office wants more details than I can remember."

"Don't forget your hard hats," said Norman, passing them out as he led the way to the mine shaft. They all trooped into the first level bate room, with its bare necessities.

"Not really much to look at here," said Philips. "Norman and I will pop down to the next level, and I'll make a few more notes."

"We will be just fine here," said Jones.

Norman and Philips headed off to the next level, leaving Jones and Helen to themselves.

"Let's give this place a thorough going over," said Jones.

"I'll check these cupboards first," said Helen. She opened each door carefully and searched every shelf. The cupboards were indeed bare. "Nothing at all here."

"No, and I've found absolutely nothing, either," said Jones, who had carefully gone over the rest of the room. "The whole place is, as you say, bare."

"Let's just sit here and wait for the others to return," said Helen.

It wasn't long before Norman and Philips returned. "Find anything?" inquired Philips.

"Nothing at all," said Jones.

As they stood up to go, Jones pointed to Helen's small handbag.

"Don't leave that behind," he called.

Helen turned around to pick up her handbag, which had fallen on the floor. "Ouch!" she yelped. "Something bit me."

"Let's have a look," said Jones, taking her hand. "Hardly a scratch."

Philips also came to look at her hand. "Nothing to see," he said.

"Let's get out of here," said Helen, beginning to really dislike the mine. The four of them returned to the lift and ascended to ground level.

As they walked to their respective vehicles, Philips said, "I'll contact you tonight when I've received instructions from the home office."

"Not too early, then, in the morning?" said Jones. "Helen could do with a long lie-in. The fresh air is knocking her out." Jones drove swiftly away from the mine, not expressing to Helen his concern for her. They arrived at the hotel hoping for a relaxing evening, but it was not to be. As they entered the Lambton Worm, Jackie was on hand to greet them.

"You don't look too well, missus," he said.

"You know, you are right," said Helen, who promptly fainted.

Jones caught her as she fell and gently lowered her onto the carpet. He took her pulse and found it to be racing. There were signs of perspiration on her forehead. Jones knew immediately what he was up against. He had seen it all before. This was snakebite.

"Is the missus alreet?" asked Jackie.

"We appear to have a problem," said Jones. "I need to use your phone." Leaving Jackie to watch over Helen, he rushed away to phone Philips. "It's happened again," he began. "Helen has gone down with snakebite. Get me a medical team over here on the double, and I mean now."

He returned to Helen, and together with Jackie carried her up to the room. He made her comfortable in bed, and then he waited. Helen came around for a few minutes and then lapsed into unconsciousness.

21

The medical team arrived a few moments later. Jones hovered nearby as they endeavored to diagnose Helen's condition. He indicated to them the likelihood of snakebite. Heeding his advice, they injected Helen with an anti-venom serum and awaited developments.

The evening drew on, and a lovely sunset glowed through the window in their room.

"What a beautiful view," thought Jones to himself, "and Helen is missing it. She might miss it forever if she doesn't come through this present danger."

Helen's condition seemed to ease, and she gradually emerged from her coma.

"How are you feeling, my dear?" Jones asked.

"I just…just can't focus my thoughts," said Helen in a weary, little voice.

"Just rest. We won the battle last time, and we can do it again," said Jones, referring to Helen's previous battle with snakebite.

She closed her eyes, and Jones continued to watch over

her like a hawk. Before long, her condition again began to deteriorate. More serum was injected. Again Helen rallied and recovered consciousness.

"I don't like it," said Jones to his wife. "You are not shaking this off."

"Do what you feel best, dear," said Helen. "My life is in your hands." She held on for awhile, then slipped away again into unconsciousness.

The medical team knew that they were beaten. They, too, had fought this very fight for miners' lives and lost. Apart from applying the serum, there was nothing they could do to win the battle for Helen's life.

"There is one more avenue we could explore, if you want to save my wife's life," said Jones to the medical team. "I need volunteers to assist me—preferably men who have faith in God."

"We all believe in God," said the captain in charge of the team. "We would have lost many a patient if it wasn't for prayer."

"Well then, that should make a difference," said Jones.

"First, let's give Helen one more shot of serum. Then, we are going to need some ice, and plenty of it. One of you can go and get another bedside lamp."

22

The team scattered to deal with their assigned tasks. A number of ice packs were prepared and assembled. The bedside lights were adjusted to create a powerful beam. Then Helen, responding to the serum, rallied again.

The team had been told exactly what was expected of them. They had failed to overcome the snakebite injuries before, and so they were very keen to win this battle with the same enemy confronting them. They had been shown the miniature and told of its purpose. They were all prepared to see this thing through to the bitter end.

Helen began to stir.

"The time has come, gentlemen, to test your faith," said Jones. "Apply the ice packs." Two of them did as they were told. Helen stirred even more. "Adjust the lamps. Focus them on the miniature, like this."

Next, Jones shouted at Helen, "Helen! Helen, wake up. Wake up!" He shook her shoulders. "Helen! Helen! Open your eyes. Can you hear me?"

"I can hear you," said Helen. "Why are you shouting?"

"Open your eyes." Her eyes fluttered open and then shut again. "Helen you've got to open your eyes. Open them, now." Her eyes opened. "Look at the serpent," commanded Jones. "Come on, Helen, look at the serpent." Her eyes remained open, trying to focus. "That's it. Keep looking at the serpent." Helen's eyes seemed to focus briefly on the miniature. The reflected light pierced her consciousness. Power emanated from the serpent. It held her transfixed for a moment or two, then slowly she slipped back into unconsciousness.

The lamps were returned to their places, and the ice packs were adjusted. Jones carefully put the miniature away. The medical team looked on in amazement, as they tried to absorb what they had just witnessed. A man had just entrusted the life of his wife to a glimpse of a snake!

"Now would be a good time to pray," said Jones to the men.

And so they waited. Some of the team did pray, and others just waited and watched. After a half an hour, a marked change came over Helen. Her breathing became easier, and her pulse rate dropped.

"She's going to make it," said the captain. "Now I really do believe in miracles."

There was a quiet tap on the door. Jones responded to it.

"How is she?" asked Jackie. "Is there anything I can do?"

"She is recovering nicely, thanks," said Jones. "It's been a close run. Tell you what, we could do with a bottle of whisky and some glasses. Tonight, we need to celebrate."

"Nee problem at all," said Jackie, who disappeared and then reappeared very shortly carrying glasses and whisky on a tray.

"Come in and share this bottle with us," Jones invited. "We are celebrating a great victory."

"I don't mind if I do," said Jackie, gleefully entering the party.

23

Philips rang Jones early the next morning. "Glad to hear that Helen is making a good recovery. Quite a fright for you both."

"It's over now," responded Jones. "We Joneses never seem to learn, do we?"

"You had better take the day off and take care of your good lady," said Philips. "I've got a squad of sound men here, and we are going to have a look at what is behind that wall."

"Don't take any risks," warned Jones. "And whatever you do, make sure that everyone wears gloves. Then snakebite will be the least of your problems."

"I hear you! See you tomorrow then," said Philips. Ever conscious of his past failures, he muttered to himself, "It's my turn now to do something spectacular." He hurried out to his assembled men. The soldiers were standing at ease when Philips addressed them. Beside him waited four mine safety officers, who looked decidedly uncomfortable.

"Today, I want two volunteers to accompany me down into the mine," said Philips. Immediately, two men came to attention and took a step forward. The other two men would spend the remainder of the day on boring guard duty for their slow response. "Carry loaded weapons," continued Philips. "We are not sure what we may find."

The volunteers checked and readied their weapons. The safety officers, equipped with small pick axes and short shovels, followed behind Philips and his volunteers. As they moved across the site to the pit head, Norman hovered about them in his usual manner. Each man was issued with a hard hat. Two of them were asked to carry powerful torches. They all entered the lift cage, which descended to level two. There was a faint smell of smoke, but otherwise everything seemed normal. They moved quietly along the seam until they came to the sealed off section.

"Any comment about the condition of this wall?" asked Philips.

"It looks set to collapse," responded a torch bearer.

"A real botched job," came another response after torch-light scrutiny.

"It must have been thrown up in a bit of a hurry," added a third voice.

"Can you think of any reason, safety-wise, that we shouldn't break through this wall?" asked Philips.

"No fire danger, that's for sure," said the leader of the safety officers.

"Let's do it then," said Philips.

The safety officers carefully picked away at the top of the wall, first removing small, then larger pieces of brick and cement. Eventually they created a gap that the men could just step through. Focusing their torches on the way ahead, the group edged slowly forward. Little wisps of smoke curled past them.

"No danger of any explosion here," said the leader. "Not much gas to speak of."

"What do you recommend as our next step?" asked Philips, wanting to keep the group involved with the decision-making.

"There is just a bit of smoke coming this way," said the leader again. "But I think we can press on without much bother. It looks safe."

"Yes, I agree," said Philips. They moved ahead slowly.

"The seam is well supported," someone commented.

"Poor quality coal," another said. As they moved cautiously forward, the smoke was noticeably increasing.

"Is it getting brighter, or am I imagining things?" Philips asked the group.

"Definitely brighter," Norman confirmed.

"And noisier," responded Philips.

Suddenly, there was a loud, roaring noise, which subsided just as quickly.

"What the heck was that?" asked Norman with alarm.

"Better wait a moment while I go on ahead to investigate," said Philips. He indicated to his two soldiers that they should come with him. The others waited as the trio edged slowly forward. The noise became louder and clearer.

"Sounds like a Bunsen burner," said the corporal.

They crept very slowly forward another thirty yards. The passage took a sharp turn to the left, and as the trio turned the corner, they were amazed to see a huge snakelike creature hardly thirty yards ahead of them.

"Down!" commanded Philips, and all three fell to the ground. They had not been observed by the creature. The serpent appeared to emanate fire and smoke from an area just below its mouth. The trio gazed incredulously at the creature before them.

"Quickly! You take the others back to the surface," Philips commanded the corporal, who responded immediately. As he departed, his movement was noticed by the creature. It turned slowly and began to gather its strength. Slowly, it moved toward Philips and his companion, and then suddenly it galvanized itself and began moving quickly forward with an awkward lunging motion.

"Open fire!" Philips ordered the other soldier, but the soldier was totally transfixed, unable to respond. "Open fire, man!" Philips yelled. He grabbed the rifle and proceeded to fire at the creature's head. The bullets had no marked effect. "Run! Run!" shouted Philips.

The other soldier came to his senses and, turning from the awful sight, ran blindly to the rear. Philips, covering the retreat, kept firing as he slowly moved back along the passage. The creature, spewing fire, was gathering momentum. Philips turned to run, but found total darkness, as the last torchbearer had evacuated before him. He ran straight into a stony outcrop and fell to the ground. The glow from the creature drew nearer. He got up and stumbled further along the wall at the end of the section. He turned to fire once more, but the creature advanced unchecked. He tried to run, but his legs would not carry him. He fired until the weapon could speak no more. Philips fell, rose, and fell again, and this time the creature was upon him. He screamed, and then his voice fell silent.

The corporal, as he was ordered, had gathered up the safety officers and departed through the gap in the wall. He sent the others to the lift while he awaited the return of Philips at the gap. The other soldier came out blindly stumbling. The corporal held him there for a moment, until the scream from Philips sent them both racing to the lift. They threw themselves into the waiting cage and ascended to the surface. There was an all-around sigh of relief as the group reached sunlight. They were met by the two soldiers who were on duty.

"Where's Major Philips?" one asked.

"Never you mind," said the corporal. "Get on that gate and let no one through. No one goes in or out." The corporal spoke next to the safety officers. "No one can leave this site until we have this problem sorted out. You can use the office over there. And you," he said addressing the soldier who had seen the creature. "I want you with me at all times. Got it?" The soldier nodded sheepishly. Norman shepherded the safety officers to the designated office.

"Now, what do I do next?" the corporal said to himself. He went into Philip's office and found a list of phone numbers. "Major Jones—he's the next in command here. I'll give him a ring."

Once he had apprised Jones of the situation, he turned his thoughts to the other soldier who had witnessed the amazing scene. "Now, tell me all about it," he said to the waiting man.

24

Meanwhile, Jones had been on the phone to the home office to inform them of the seriousness of the situation at Old Smokey. He picked out the salient facts from the corporal's garbled story, but Jones made it clear that there was a critical situation at the mine needing heavy and comprehensive reinforcements.

Jones, confident that Helen was making a good recovery, left the medical team to watch over her while he hurried to Old Smokey. Upon his arrival, he was met by locked mine gates, which took a few moments to re-open.

"Sorry about the delay," said the corporal. "No one is being allowed in or out."

"No sign of Major Philips?" asked Jones.

"None, sir," responded the corporal, relieved to have a senior officer take the responsibility off his shoulders.

"Go and bring the other soldier who was involved," said Jones. "I want you both to go over the whole set of events again from the beginning, leaving nothing out."

They moved to Philip's office where they went thoroughly over every detail. Later, Jones interviewed the safety officers, but his conversation with them revealed nothing new, and clearly they had not seen the creature. The description the soldiers gave of the creature was so far beyond belief, that Jones decided he must see the thing for himself. He was just thinking about his next step when he heard a sharp clattering noise. A light army tank had rolled straight through the locked mine gates, smashing them. The tank was closely followed by three trucks loaded with men and munitions. The Durham Light Infantry had arrived. A sprightly young major leapt from the tank, marched up to Jones, and saluted.

"Major Jones? Having a spot of bother, are we, sir?"

"You could say that, major," said Jones, returning his salute in a half-hearted manner.

"Major Hughes, Second Battalion. G.H.Q. sent me up here on the double. What exactly is the problem, sir?"

"We have a serious situation here, Hughes. The first thing we need to do is secure the perimeter. The tank entrance was a bit heavy handed, don't you think?" said Jones referring to the smashed gate. "But you do have the right idea."

"Sorry about that, sir."

"We need the pit head area totally sealed off."

Hughes moved his vehicles into position and then stationed his own men, supported by the tank, at the pit head building.

"This could be very messy," said Jones. "We need armed volunteers to go with us down into the mine."

"What exactly are we up against?" asked Hughes. "Terrorists?"

"Could be much more than we have bargained for," said

Jones. "I have to tell you, before we go any further, there may well be some sort of a creature down there."

"Creature?"

"Could well be," added Jones. "I must tell you that Major Philips may be dead as a result of its aggression."

"Philips dead?"

"We won't know for sure until we get in there, so let's get to it."

Hughes addressed his assembled soldiers. "We have a dangerous situation down below. Those going in must be armed. Volunteers for this mission fall out to the lift over there." All eight of those not already assigned to a task fell out and moved quickly over to the pit head.

"Quite impressive!" commented Jones.

"It's what you expect from the Durham Light Infantry."

"What have you brought in your support vehicles?"

"We have a wide variety of weaponry," said Hughes. "You name it, we have it."

"We will need grenades, explosives, and possibly a flame thrower, if you have one," said Jones.

"We do have a modern flame thrower, but I doubt whether anyone has actually used one before. One of my men has the qualifications to use it, so it will be up to him," said Hughes.

"Better warn him now," said Jones.

Hughes had a word with the soldier, and then he detailed two soldiers to collect the weaponry. A satchel containing hand grenades was also brought from the support vehicle. Once assembled, the group of soldiers was divided in two. Norman reappeared from his office to issue everyone with hard hats. Torches were also handed out. Norman himself carried a short pick.

"You might need one of these," he said. "I'll bring it doon." Clearly Norman was coming, whether the officers liked it or not.

Jones took charge of the first squad to go down in the cage, and Hughes followed behind with the second squad. Jones's squad emerged cautiously from the cage. Level two was quiet, with not even a hint of smoke. He gestured for the men to move forward. They advanced about thirty yards and then stopped as the noise of the returning cage reached their ears. Hughes's squad was allowed to join up, and together they moved forward. They found their way to the broken wall.

"Here is where we need to get organized," said Jones.

"This gap needs enlarging if we are to move freely through it," said Hughes.

"Let me do it," said Norman, who hacked into the wall with gusto using his pick. The stones fell from the wall, and a cloud of cement dust began to cover the soldiers. He quickly created a gap wide enough for two people to pass through comfortably

"Better tidy this mess up," said Hughes. "We don't want to fall over these stones."

His men quickly sorted out a clear pathway.

"Can I suggest that the flame thrower be situated here?" said Jones, indicating a position twenty meters short of the broken wall. Hughes spoke to the soldiers in charge of the weapon, and they prepared it for use, settling into the rear of the small section of wall that Norman had left standing.

"Norman, I want you to stay here behind these men," said Jones. Then turning to Hughes he said, "We will need two good men up front."

Hughes responded, "Smith and Copley, check your weapons and take the lead."

"These need to go into safe hands," said Jones, referring to the hand grenades.

Hughes handed the satchel to a lance corporal and said, "Prepare yourself to use these on my command." The lance corporal opened the satchel and checked its contents.

"No problem here, sir," he responded.

"I want you beside me, ready to act when I give the word," said Hughes.

"Let's be moving in then," said Jones.

The men in the lead had already moved slowly into the section, but they had come to a standstill. Hughes joined them. "What is it?" Then he noticed that the pair was examining a rifle and an officer's cap lying on the ground.

Jones joined them, "Philips?"

"Philips," responded Hughes. Nothing else needed to be said.

Very cautiously the group moved on, with Smith and Copley leading the way. They heard a noise that sounded like a controlled roar. Then, the mine appeared to be growing lighter. The men hardly dared to breathe with the suspense. The awareness of danger was overwhelming. There was a faint smell of smoke. Smith and Copley dropped to the floor. The others stood and waited.

Copley crawled forward, and Smith followed a few yards behind. Turning the corner of the gallery, Copley was shocked to behold the creature. It was bigger now, not that Copley knew why. Smith crawled up alongside him. He, too, was overawed at the sight. The creature was emitting a bright fire. Together they withdrew and reported the amazing sight to Hughes.

"It's a monster, sir," said Copley.

"It's bloody big, sir," said Smith.

"Grenades, then?" Hughes suggested.

"What about capturing it for a zoo?" offered Jones.

"Not really the time for frivolity," said Hughes.

"Let the two of us go forward and take a look," suggested Jones.

"Yes, we should do that," said Hughes. "I want to see this thing, anyway." Hughes and Jones crawled forward until they could see the creature. It sensed their presence immediately and began to stir. Shuffling back to the others, Hughes said to the lance corporal, "Ready with those grenades?"

The corporal moved forward, preparing to throw the grenades that were already in his hands. As he turned the corner of the seam, he saw the creature moving slowly toward him. He fumbled nervously with the pins and then rolled the grenades in the direction of the giant snake. Then, he retreated quickly and joined Hughes. The grenades exploded, creating a deafening sound and bringing a great roar from the creature. The light intensified in the passage where the soldiers stood. The creature was on the move.

"Two more grenades from here," ordered Hughes. The grenades were rolled to the point where the gallery turned. "Everyone fall back!" shouted Hughes. Jones and the others hurried away. The grenades exploded with another deafening sound and produced a second mighty roar from the creature. The men moved even further to the rear of the section.

"You two," said Hughes to Smith and Copley. "Take up firing positions."

The creature came around the corner, moving with increasing velocity toward them. Smith and Copley began to open fire with their rifles. The creature continued on unchecked.

"Fall back!" shouted Hughes. Turning to the lance corporal, he said, "Prepare to launch grenades." Smith and Copley raced past Hughes. "Grenades!" yelled Hughes, as the creature loomed ever closer. The grenades were rolled forward.

The noise of the explosion plus the noise of outrage from the creature was deafening. "Run like heck!" ordered Hughes. The three of them scrambled down the gallery as fast as they could, with the beast lunging at them. They reached the breach in the wall and hurled themselves through the enlarged gap.

"Open fire!" ordered Hughes.

The defenders of the breach were well-prepared and delivered withering firepower upon the creature. It stopped and drew back for a moment, just around the curve of the gallery.

"Cease fire!" commanded Hughes. In the short silence that followed, the men could hear the creatures roar beginning to build.

"What on earth is it doing now?" asked Jones.

Suddenly, Jones remembered the dream, the dragon, and the lance pinning its rear leg to the ground. Perhaps it was some divine inspiration on how to stop the monster.

"Did you notice that the creature has a pair of rather short rear legs?" he asked Hughes.

"No, I didn't." said Hughes.

"When it comes at us again, I suggest that we direct fire at the left leg," said Jones. "Firing at random doesn't appear to do any good."

"Good idea. The two of us can concentrate on that area," said Hughes.

The roaring increased, and the creature reappeared around the corner. The men fired their rifles, but with little effect. Hughes and Jones targeted the left leg, but the creature advanced unchecked.

"So much for my dream," muttered Jones to himself.

"Fall back everyone," said Hughes. "Fall back with me. Get well beyond our next position, where the flame thrower is situated. Prepare the flamethrower!"

The soldiers moved back, with Smith and Copley continuing to provide cover fire. The beast was within ten yards of the breach when the pair turned and ran. There was a tremendous roar, as it hurled itself against the breach. The creature thrashed and struggled to break through.

"Aim your weapon," Hughes commanded the flamethrower crew. "Prepare to fire on my command. Major Jones, I want you to take Norman and two of my men back to the surface as fast as you can. We will follow as soon as we are able." Jones and Norman fell back immediately. "All set?" Hughes inquired of the crew.

"Ready, sir," was the response.

A fierce roar heralded the creature breaking through the last remnants of the wall. It was now entering the main gallery and plunging toward the remaining soldiers.

"Fire!" yelled Hughes.

The flamethrower sputtered to life and then delivered a full discharge. Flames reached out toward the oncoming creature. Initially, it came on heedlessly into the blaze. Then, all at once it seemed to realize the intensity of the flames being hurled against it. The creature checked itself, slowing down its forward impetus. The flames continued to beat upon it, and the creature began to suffer and backed awkwardly away from the torment. It roared, but this time it was roaring with pain. The flame-thrower suddenly stopped working.

"It's all used up, sir," said the lance corporal. "There's no reserve with it, either."

"Let's get in and finish the job," said Hughes. He called forward all of his remaining men on level two. "Grenades and rifles ready. We are going to finish it off."

They moved up the gallery once more. The creature was nowhere in sight. They spotted it trying to squirm its way back through the breach in the wall.

"Open fire!" Hughes shouted. Firepower was held on the creature, as it continued to fight its way through the breach. As it disappeared down into its own gallery, grenades followed to hasten its retreat. The soldiers maintained pressure on the retreating animal until it reached its lair. The remaining grenades were delivered, and rifle fire was poured down upon the creature. "Keep firing," ordered Hughes, as the men confronted the creature.

The beast ceased its noise. It appeared to be dead.

"Cease fire," Hughes said. "Stay alert for any other creatures."

All was quiet. The soldiers surveyed the scene. Where on earth had this creature come from? What did it live on? What kind of creature was it? Were there others like it? Where was its mate? The soldiers looked around apprehensively. If the creature's mate appeared now, they were lost!

Hughes broke the silence, "Time to move out." His men turned to leave, but Hughes corrected them. "Not like that! Have you men learned nothing about warfare? Fall back in pairs. Smith and Copley, cover us."

They edged slowly away from the fallen enemy and the scene of devastation. Once they reached the breach in the wall, Hughes allowed them to turn and take one final look at the scene. After a short interval, they moved quickly to the lift.

25

As they emerged into the bright sunlight, a concerned Jones greeted them. "Glad to see that you have survived. I was getting worried about you."

"Well, we killed the creature," said Hughes in cocky tone. "So, what do you want us to do next?"

"Look for other creatures."

"What other creatures?" was the startled response.

"I had better fill you in on the real problem here," said Jones. He took Hughes to one side and recounted the events of the past few days. "So you see, there is another threat lingering in the mine."

"I see," said Hughes. "But could it be that both problems are related? Was the large creature of the same species as the snakes you talk about?"

"We just don't know, unless the larger one turned cannibal."

"That is a possibility," agreed Hughes. "So there could still be lots of small snakes in the mine?"

"Exactly," said Jones. "What we need to do is to wipe out the lot of them."

"I don't know how it can be done," said Hughes. "We only have a certain amount of explosives with us."

"There is an alternative," said Jones. "We could poison them."

"How can we do that?" Hughes looked skeptically at Jones.

"Each mine has a dangerous goods store. We may be able to use whatever Norman has in his stores to cleanse the mine of its residents."

"I'll take a look," said Hughes. Norman was summoned and made to reveal the exact contents of the store.

"There's nee gannin into that store withoot gloves on, ye understand?"

"He's right about that," said Jones. "We need to handle all of the chemicals and substances very carefully."

"Then blow the whole thing up," responded Hughes. "I get the picture."

Hughes, with Norman hovering over him, gathered his men together and informed them of the final act of destruction. Gloves were distributed, helmets checked, and instructions given on the placing of chemicals and explosives. After three hours of work, the mine was prepared for the final detonation of charges. Hughes disappeared again into the mine with his corporal for a final check. He reappeared moments later, giving the thumbs up signal to the soldier appointed to set off the detonation. The soldiers, officials, and of course, Norman, were gathered around Jones. There was a slight ground tremor, and that was all. They looked in wonder at the pit head, as a huge column of smoke rose into the air. Within a few minutes, the smoke took on a thin, wispy appearance. "That's Auld Smokey," said Norman.

"Your attention, men," Jones began. "What you have seen and heard on this site is top secret. If you have any problems concerning today's action, you may contact the number I will give you before you leave. Do not, I repeat, do not disclose to anyone what you have witnessed today. If you do, the home office will deny all knowledge of you, and some of you may find that your pensions are cut."

The miners, in particular, looked at each other. That was hitting where it hurt. Getting drunk one night and spilling their story could cost them their pension. They would have to be teetotalers from then on.

"I repeat, there was never any such thing as the Lambton Worm. It is only a legend. Any living creatures in the mine have been totally incinerated. This mine will be closed up and never entered again—not even by Norman!"

The squad of soldiers that had remained above ground and had not been involved in the fighting was put on guard duty by Hughes. All of the other soldiers were loaded onto army trucks and driven away. Hughes would have the difficult task of debriefing them, and, making out his official report would be a real headache. There was no way he could tell the truth about the action in Old Smokey that day. The other officials were gently ushered away from the site by Norman.

Jones acknowledged the salute from the men at the gate as he drove away, but he noted a thin wisp of smoke still rising from the mine in his rearview mirror.

"I hope that this is the last time I see Old Smokey," he

muttered to himself. "What on earth will I tell Helen? There is no deceiving a woman."

Helen was up and about, awaiting his return. She looked very relieved to see him enter the room. "What was the emergency?" she asked.

"Had a bit of trouble on level two," Jones responded. "But Hughes and I fixed it. We burned out the snakes on both levels, and we put out the fire in Old Smokey for good. The job is done. We can go home as soon as you feel well enough to travel."